'Death Lurks in Cock Muck Hill'

The Borough Boys
Book two

A Novella

By Phil Simpkin

To Kate

With my very best wishes

Phil.

xxx

Contents

Cock Muck Hill, Leicester, March 1851.....................7

Chapter One – Monday 3rd March 1851 10

Chapter Two – 'Showing the flag' 20

Chapter Three – 'Lines in the sand' 29

Chapter Four – 'A turn for the worse' 39

Chapter Five – 'The Rats' Castle'.............................46

Chapter Six – 'A mischief of Rats'............................53

Chapter Seven – 'A blast from the past'.................62

Chapter Eight – 'Long live the King'........................73

Chapter Nine – 'No such thing as a free breakfast'82

Chapter Ten – 'Rats on the run'...............................87

Chapter Eleven – 'A return to normality?'.............95

Copyright Information

Acknowledgements

This book would not have been possible without my 'little band of helpers'.

Thanks to my long suffering wife (and editor in chief) for being so objective!

Thanks also to Dave & Mel; Anne S; Annie C; Lian; Megan and Roger, for their additional proof reading & feedback.

Thank you guys!

About the Author

Phil Simpkin is a retired Police Officer and now spends his spare time writing. He is a keen local history and genealogy practitioner, and his interests have given him an insight into old Leicester, which has proven to be invaluable to him in writing this series.

Phil's first novel in The Borough Boys series, 'Jack Ketch's Puppets', was published earlier in 2013.

This novella is the second part of that series, and two further novellas are planned for later this year, to take Samson Shepherd, John Beddows and The Borough Boys up to 1854 when the next *full* novel is set.

Phil has also recently published 'Leicestershire Myth & Legend – in verse', a series of short verse that covers the folklore, myth and legend of the City and County, in his own, unique, way.

Contemporary novels featuring Detective Tony Lawrence are under construction and the first novel in that series will be available shortly.

More information as to where and how you can obtain Phil's books is available at the end of this book.

'The Rookeries'

For those of you who are unfamiliar with the setting in this series of novels and novellas, view my 'Borough Boys' page, where I describe them further, at my website...

http://www.1455bookcompany.com/the-borough-boys.html

Cock Muck Hill. Sunday 2nd March 1851.

Aggie Black sat crouched over the small candle, wearily darning one of an old pair of socks. The fat wax stump had been well used, and she might just have enough light from it, for one or two more days. Only the few flames from the small fire in her grate gave her the extra light by which she could see; enough heat to keep her gnarled fingers free enough to complete the now difficult task. No more coal was due for a week or two, and she had to make it last.

That being said, Aggie was better off than most, as she had a son, Porky – as he was most commonly known - who visited. A butcher and slaughterer by trade; he always brought her a few roughly made sausages, from his trimmings, or a bit of boiled pig's trotter or a left-over pig's ear, unlike the other occupants. Many had not seen meat for years, so poor were they.

Provided 'free gratis' by the Parish Guardians and only for the poorest of the poor, the almshouses were a small piece of sanctity for their ragged occupants; a shabby and often leaking roof over their heads and five hundredweight of coal each year to keep them warm. The old folk, all whiling their dotage away, needed a candle - or candles - if they were more fortunate, almost all the time, owing to the constant, claustrophobic darkness within which they were contained.

'What in God's name now?' cried out the nervous, frail, old woman as something crashed through the small window, facing out onto the tiny courtyard which backed onto the rear of the almshouses, sending remnants of the four glass panels that had until then been held together with leaded strips, flying into the small area in which Aggie sat.

What appeared to be a length of wood, perhaps a table leg, crashed momentarily into Mother Black's cramped scullery, closely followed by a bloodied face, large and set with a look of fear, with somebody else's hand and strong forearm visible behind it, pushing it down onto the broken remnants of glass and frame.

'Feckin' bastard, lct go of mc, oil fcckin kill yers,' shouted the man with the bloodied face.

Outside, the sound of men and women screaming, temporarily drowned out any other noise, as English, Irish, Scottish and Welsh fought one another, in another of the now common place street battles that had broken out across the patchwork of tiny streets, alleyways and courtyards that made up 'The Rookeries'.

These street battles had become increasingly bloody, and had been raging since April fool's day 1850, when Dubh O'Donnell and his cronies had received their just rewards at the hands of William Calcraft, at the Gallows, outside the County Gaol.

Assumptions that 'The Rookeries' would fall into the hands of Sean Crowley and what was left of O'Donnell's 'bruisers', had proved unfounded. Dubh O'Donnell's empire had slipped into insignificance; Crowley had not been seen or heard of since.

Tonight, the Irish population was taking a heavy beating and with what was left of the resident 'bruisers', some new gang was taking the upper hand in the area; the Irish, seemingly unable to put them down, or even compete at their level of violence. The strong arm tactics of the large Irish population in the recent past was no longer the predominant force, and it was now survival of the fittest or strongest, whoever and however that may be!

For Head Constable Robert Charters of The Borough Police, the reality was that a strength of just fifty or so men to Police the area all day, every day, was grossly inadequate, thus, even the smaller gangs that were now vying for a position in the pecking order outnumbered them by several to one.

So, many new 'players' were trying their hand at ruling the roost amongst the poverty, vice, drunkenness and crime that formed daily life for the overcrowded population.

It would take something or someone, harder or more menacing, to stop them in their tracks.

Chapter One – Monday 3rd March 1851

Detective Sergeant Herbert Kettle had desperately tried to avoid the blooded and smelly slaughter-man, Porky Black, but had missed his brief opportunity to slip out of the side door of 'The Artilleryman' pub and into the crowds of Humberstone Gate.

'Mister Kettle, so glad I caught you,' said Porky. 'What are you lot doing about these gangs, down in The Rookeries?'

'We're doing our damnedest, Porky, me old duck,' said Kettle, mentally gagging at the man's putrid stench, 'but this is almost open warfare. We don't have the numbers to do anything more than try to stop it spreading outside of the Rookeries, at present.'

'Last night me old Ma's house got trashed. Some Paddy's face was nearly cut off and left on her window sill. Frightened her to death, it did,' said Porky. 'We've been talking about sorting it out ourselves. All the local boys, from the slaughter houses and butchers; we'd soon sort it out. More than can be said of your lot.'

'It doesn't need any extra help from you lot. Can you imagine if it spilled up into the town as well? They'll come out of their alleys and find you, give them half a chance,' said Kettle.

'Well the boys have asked me to let you know, Mr Kettle. If it ain't sorted soon, then there'll be a real war on your hands. You can't say you ain't been warned. The locals aren't happy and you lot are standing around, or supping in the back of pubs while it's all going on, turning a blind eye.'

'Porky; you tell your mates that if we want their help, we'll come and ask for it. Just keep them calm. Wait and see what we can do next,' said Kettle, mindful that all the eyes in pub were now upon him, aware that Porky had become quite loud.

Even though today, Kettle might serve a purpose for them, he still felt conspicuous. Detectives were seen as the ultimate 'nosey' and the customers of this particular pub were well known for 'manhandling' them out if they felt threatened, as others had found out, to their cost.

'Suppose a beer's out of the question?' chuckled Porky.

'If it stops a war, it might just be worth it,' said Kettle, reaching in his jacket pocket for a couple of pennies.

*****

Robert Charters sat behind his office desk, just off the muster room, at the rear of the Town Hall Station, hands clasped behind his head. With him in the room stood Herbert Kettle, 'Tanky' Smith, 'Black Tommy' Haynes, and John Beddows - all of his finest detectives.

'So, what do you suggest we do to stop this disorder? Don't want the Militia or The Riot Act, if we can avoid it!' said Charters, looking to his men for answers.

'Trouble is, sir, we've got so many gangs now, all without a clear edge over the other, that nobody is taking control and sorting it out. Since Dubh O'Donnell got necked, it's gone from bad to worse. The Irish are getting their arses kicked routinely, which is unheard of,' said Tanky Smith.

'We have got a foot in quite a few doors now, and every gang is saying the same. The only thing that is stopping us is someone taking the bull by the horns and taking overall control,' said Tommy Haynes.

'I thought that Sean Crowley was going to take over in the Rookeries and his boys would carry on as before. It might have been rough, but at least the Irish had that level of control,' said Beddows.

'And where is Sean Crowley? Why hasn't he taken over the empire?' said Charters.

'The Paddies say he is back in the '*Ole Country*' and doing rather nicely. A few big winners at the Curragh as well, so word has it! Hasn't even been back to see his Ma or Pa, not since they went down!' said Beddows. 'He has little or no interest in Leicester, or so it seems, presently at least.'

'One thing that keeps coming up is about our uniform colleagues. Nobody seems able to go in the Rookeries and stamp the trouble out when it breaks out,' said Smith. 'Tommy and me keep having a sly pop at a few, but we can't be there all that much, with everything else that's going on.'

'So what do we do?' said Charters. 'What if we double up the constables and put two down there all the time; regular men, instead of leaving dead wood or rotten apples down there?'

'That would be a start. The ones that are there at the moment are weak, or have had their bellyful. We could do with some new blood down there, someone with the stomach for a fight!' said Haynes.

'Put Shepherd down there,' said Beddows. 'He's doing a grand job around the Town Centre and getting well respected. He can talk to people that others can't. But he is also a hard young bugger and hungry still.'

'Who else?' said Charters.

'What about young Perkins?' said Beddows. 'He does a bit of boxing, so I understand. He and Shepherd are getting matey and often sparring in their time off.'

'When are they next on duty?' said Charters.

'They start nights, tonight; nine o'clock,' said Beddows. 'Right then, Smith and Haynes; I want you to give them the good news, and to tell them who and what you know at the moment - the gangs; the leaders, and so on;

where to go; where to tread carefully, that sort of stuff. They can make a start down there as of tonight!' said Charters.

'Yes, sir,' said Tanky Smith.

'Poor bleeders; I used to hate it down there when I was younger, day in, day out; constantly watching over your shoulder. This will make or break them. We can cover their backs as much as we can, but we also have other duties to attend to,' said Beddows.

'We can try,' said Smith, 'but the rest is down to them. As you say, they're feisty young pups.'

*****

Shortly before nine o'clock, Samson Shepherd strolled in to the Police Station on Town Hall Lane.

Much to the amusement of everyone gathered for 'Parade', Shepherd was sporting a rather dark, but otherwise colourful 'black eye', which had certainly not been there at the end of duty the previous morning.

'Told you not to upset young Sally,' said Beddows, with a beaming grin, lighting up the gloom. 'How did you miss that one?'

'As it happens, it wasn't the lovely Sally at all. It was that rather fleet-footed dodger, ducker and diver, Perkins. Little bleeder caught me right off-guard!'

As he spoke, in walked the cocky young Constable Perkins, the latest addition to Shepherd's shift.

'Constable Perkins,' came the booming voice from behind the Charge Desk.

'We need every man fit and well on nights, yet I understand that you have tried to reduce our numbers?' said Sergeant Sheffield, the Station Charge Sergeant on duty, as he always seemed to be, customarily drawing on his favourite clay pipe.

'Getting a bit slow in his old age,' said Perkins, grinning. 'My old lady could have hit him with the one that got him!'

'When you Gentlemen have quite finished slobbering, we require your presence in Mr Charters' office, if you would be so kind,' said Beddows, running his index finger around the inside of his high collar, an old nervous trait.

'Wondered what you were doing in here at this time of night, Sarge,' said Shepherd. 'I suspect that you have something unpleasant for me, or is it just a little too warm for you tonight?'

'Not just you, Mr Shepherd. We have something for you and your cocky young sparring partner, or rather, Charters has! Sergeant; can you explain to the Night Sergeants that Messrs Shepherd and Perkins will join them shortly, and they will be out with the rest of the shift as expected. But only when Mr Charters has properly advised them of their task?' said Beddows.

'Last time Mr Shepherd got *special dispensation* for his duties, half of Leicester got murdered. Hope it ain't a déjà vu moment?' said a bemused Sheffield, twisting the ends of his moustache to fine points, between closed fingers, whilst peering over the top his pince-nez.

*****

Gathered in Mr Charters' office were Sergeants Smith, Haynes, Kettle and now Beddows, together with Mr Charters himself.

'Come in and shut the door,' said Charters, looking up from some scribbled notes he was making. 'Good God Shepherd, whatever has happened to your face?'

'Bumped into one of Constable Perkins right jabs, I'm embarrassed to admit,' said Shepherd.

'Not a good omen, for what I have in mind for you both,' said Charters, rolling his eyes upwards and shaking his head. 'I have a little job, which needs two, tough young men, prepared to take a few risks and sort out a rather hostile and growing problem we have. You two have been personally recommended by each of these fine detectives, for some reason!'

'That's very thoughtful of them, sir,' said Shepherd. 'Might I assume then, that there is an element of physical risk attached?'

'Doesn't every day as a constable offer a physical risk?' said Charters, smiling. No sympathy from him tonight! 'As you know, we have a problem in the Rookeries. Things are out of control and everyone is fighting with everyone else. It has to stop,' Charters continued. 'The detectives are doing all they can to get inside these gangs, and we are getting some idea now, of who is at the forefront of each faction, but nobody is gaining control and nor should they. It is our responsibility to stop them in their tracks and restore law and order down there.'

'If I might chip in for a moment, sir?' said Tanky Smith.

'Carry on, Sergeant,' said Charters.

'Everyone thought that Sean Crowley would be back by now, and that the Irish would have restored the peace, by taking back control over the damn place, but he's tucked up in Ireland, so we understand. As there is no leader willing to pull the Irish together, some new groups are springing up, and the in-fighting has now gone from bad to worse.'

'There's a new gang, The Sandacre Street Rats, who seem to be at the bottom of it, outside the Irish, that is. They're a bunch of incomers from London or thereabouts; layabouts and thieves, and mixed in are some hard Scots bastards that have settled there now, too. One or two Welsh ex soldiers also; again, hard bastards. These 'Rats' are having a go at everyone now, or so it appears,' said Haynes.

'Rumour has it that they've established a base in the old Lodging House in Bateman's Yard, off Bateman's Row. Close enough to get to the Irish, but within enough of their own sort to make it a stronghold. Now they're also trying to force out some of the Leicester locals too, as it seems they want to move more of their own into the area. Scared Porky Black's old ma and the older residents in Cock Muck Hill, half to death, the other night,' said Herbert Kettle.

'And where and how do we come in to the plans, sir?' said Shepherd.

'Your colleagues, including without doubt, some of those on your own shift, are failing to stamp on them. I don't know if it is a case of *no courage,* or whether they are being paid off to ignore it, but something has gone wrong,' said Charters.

'Tommy and I have been in the usual haunts, suitably dressed up, as we do, and seen your mates in uniform. Drinking in the back rooms, and turning a blind eye, as far as we can see. A warm hidey hole, and a few beers and they're anyone's!' said Tanky Smith. 'Mr Charters now has an idea who's reliable or not.'

'So, I am moving the regular constables on the beats that cover Mansfield Street, Abbey Street, Sandacre Street and Green Street area, and I want you two to take the beats on as your regular patrol for the next few weeks. I think I can trust you not to do what your colleagues seem to be doing?' said Charters.

'I'm up for it, sir,' said Shepherd. 'What about you Perkins?'

'If it sorts it out, I'm up for anything. Anyway, it sounds like it will save a few pennies on sparring with you for a few weeks.'

'You two will spend your entire duties down there. Anyone steps out of line, and I want you standing on their toes. Know what I mean?' said Charters.

'Mr Shepherd is very adept at standing on people's toes, sir,' said Beddows. 'He had a good mentor!'

'As I well recall, Mr Beddows; as I well recall,' said Charters.

'From tonight, you two are the only men routinely on those streets. If anyone else is seen there, it'll be to back you up, or else I'll have their crown jewels!' said Charters. 'I want hard, but fair! And you will need to be hard, believe me!'

'Yes, sir; hard, and fair!' said Shepherd. Perkins nodded quietly, in agreement.

'I will advise Sergeant Sheffield to inform all of the duty sergeants and the usual constables on those beats, that you two are there until further notice. You do your normal duty pattern, unless something happens that needs you to drop back or forward. We'll deal with that if it happens. But I want you to get a grip of the Rookeries,' said Charters.

'You'll probably see me and Tommy moving in and out of the shitholes,' said Tanky. 'Don't even think of acknowledging us, as we don't need a kicking at your expense! We'll do our bit; you do your bit. If we pop out the shadows every now and again and 'intervene' that's down to us too. Understand?'

'Yes, Sergeant,' said Shepherd.

'The Lodging House in Bateman's Yard is what they're now calling *'The Rats' Castle'*. Most of the incomers are from London, and apparently it's the name they gave to a similar shithole in their old Rookeries in St Giles. Seem to think it's funny!'

'Have you been in there yet?' said Perkins.

'Can I just say, we're working on it!' said Tanky Smith. 'None of the uniform blokes have even tried, and probably wouldn't even get into Bateman's Row, let alone Bateman's Yard without getting a kicking for their nerve!'

'Sounds like a bit of a challenge?' said Perkins.

'Don't go getting any silly notions, lad,' said Beddows. 'Don't want Mrs Shepherd blaming me for getting young Samson here a kicking *again*...or worse!'

'Don't you worry about us, Sergeant Beddows. I think The Rookeries might be in for a bit of a surprise!' said Shepherd.

*****

Archie Perkins, at seven months younger than Shepherd, was the last constable to join the Borough Force. Not quite as tall as Shepherd, with blond, almost white, hair, and shocking light blue eyes, he was wiry in build, and his uniform looked to hang off him.

With his tall stovepipe hat, he looked willowy and ungainly, but Shepherd had quickly found out that he was both mentally and physically tough and agile, could run like a deer, and seemed to have little, if any, fear. He was also a bit handy with his fists, and had joined the Police to use them against the criminals, rather than against the law. He was very secretive about his upbringing.

'Not been down The Rookeries much, yet, Shepherd. What's it really like down there, all day, every day?' enquired Perkins.

'You'll soon find out. It's not one of my favourite areas, and most of my experience down there was twelve months ago with Sergeant Beddows, when he was my mentor; spent quite a while down there whilst we investigated some murders.'

'The blokes that work down there every day, they hardly speak to any of us. Why is that?' said Perkins.

'I suspect they are so into turning a blind eye, that they are probably all taking some inducement - booze or coins - and probably keep themselves to themselves, so as not to get caught out. Rumour has it that Mr Charters has six constables on strength at present, with a total of forty reprimands for drunkenness between them; yet he can't dismiss them without the say so of the Watch Committee. He'd kick them all out if he had more evidence and Borough support.'

'How come the Sergeants don't stamp on them?' said Perkins.

'Most of the Sergeants are okay, I think. We got a good one with Sergeant Wright. Sergeant Sheffield is a good bloke too. Watch out for Waters though, he's on the other side of the shift, and is a nasty bastard, and he has the shady ones on the shift under his wing. Mr Beddows can't stand him.'

'I'm glad I'm on this side then,' replied Perkins.

'Got all your appointments? Truncheon? Rattle? Lamp?' enquired Shepherd.

'Too right, I have!' said Perkins, 'Never know when we might need them, as I hear we might, probably, down there.'

'Been for a piss?' asked Shepherd?

'What?' said Perkins, bemused.

'You'll learn,' Shepherd grinned back. 'Right, we've got a parade to muster for.'

Chapter Two – 'Showing the flag'

Amidst the clearly growing discontent of the assembled ranks, twenty-five constables of the night shift set off in a column; marching out in pairs; turning right out of Town Hall Lane, and up towards High Cross. It was mild and muggy for early March. No capes would be needed tonight.

Officers detached from the rear of the column as they arrived at the start of each beat, immediately commencing their patrol.

The two men who had previously patrolled the Rookeries were the first to be detached, one at High Cross, where in a few hours, the Grocers and Vegetable growers would flock to set up their stands and the next at High Street and Eastgates. Both looked at each other, nervously, mumbling away to the older members of the shift, wondering why they had been taken off *their* beats. Their new beats, so close to the station, would mean they would get maximum supervision, and would find it hard to avoid their duties. They would have to start all over again, tapping up old acquaintances, and finding new tea spots, or preferably somewhere for a quiet pint or three.

No doubt the rest of the shift would be calling Shepherd blind, as they also had done twelve months prior. He had acquired a nickname of 'golden trinkets' already, as he was clearly favoured by Charters and the detectives in the Borough. Once or twice he had experienced this discontent, when calling for assistance, and getting none, where for others, many would have come running. He had learned who to trust and who not to trust, very quickly. Perkins would no doubt get the same treatment.

The Column turned left, down Churchgate, and at the junction with Mansfield Street, Shepherd and Perkins detached from the remaining men, who carried on towards Burleys Lane and the edge of St Margaret's, marching in time with their Sergeant's rhythmic chant, 'left, right, left...'

*****

As normal, by nine thirty, the pubs and gin palaces were already starting to slowly fill, and Churchgate was busy. Many of the 'Girls of the Night' were wandering around, looking for a punter to sneak into an alleyway and earn a few coins; the bustles of their long dresses dragging trails in the dirt of the pavements.

Posh cabs drove slowly by, with their wheels grinding on the cobbles and grit; their horses' hooves striking rhythmically, echoing off the surrounding walls; their occupants seeking out a pretty girl or boy for a bit of gratification. The younger the better, was still sadly the norm on the streets. Manky Lil's and one or two better 'Abbeys' had learned to employ the services of the older ones, legally, at twelve and upwards.

Churchgate had started to attract quite a few 'boys of the night', and a 'Mollies only' club was reputed to be opened at the back of the Sun Inn, but it didn't cause a problem, so had been left alone by the Police, presently at least. Some interesting new cabs were to be found parked up nearby, giving a clue as to the preferences of their well heeled owners.

Down by Star Foundry, where Shepherd got a curt 'Hello,' from Malachi Harris, the Night Watchman; along into Mansfield Street, passing Short Street, and the closed yard of the dubious undertaker Mr Pawley, now care of The Borough Gaol; and by Delaney's yard, where Shepherd had found the body of Dubh O'Donnell's bruiser, slaughtered. The same sad and over-burdened old mule still stood in the yard.

'What's all the whistling and yelping?' said Perkins.

'That's the warning cry. They're announcing our arrival in the Rookeries,' said Shepherd. 'This is where and when your job changes and the promise of a bit of a rough time begins - if we are to believe our trusted detectives.'

'They won't know what's hit them; you and me down here,' said Perkins.

'Don't get too cocky, Perkins. We could get our arses kicked, so be careful. Don't rise to their taunts, and don't back down. If we get in a scrap, you watch my back, and I'll watch yours.'

'What did Sergeant Smith mean about keeping a watch on us?' said Perkins.

'Those two, Sergeants Smith and Haynes, almost live down here. These days, they're always in disguise and normally, very hard to spot. Sometimes they work alone, sometimes together. They'll have a foot in some of the doors we're going to walk through, or even kick down. So, if you think you spot either of them, ignore them. Don't do anything to put them at risk,' said Shepherd.

'How do they get away with it?' asked Perkins.

'Think of this. Tanky Smith and Black Tommy...Black and Smith! Both go together; both hard as nails! These blokes can get in anywhere, and will be doing things that have to be done, that others wouldn't dare do.'

'So what are we going to do?' said Perkins.

'We walk, and we talk. Try and get people on our side. If trouble starts, we stop it. That's the idea, anyway,' said

Shepherd. 'First port of call is Cock Muck Hill, and we'll show our faces down there. See if there's any of the old uns still up and about and make sure they're okay.'

*****

By about ten o'clock, small groups of men were hanging about on Mansfield Street.

Most groups gave the two constables suspicious or menacing stares, and the odd abuse was uttered; mainly in English, and mostly mixed in with derogatory terms that were now being coined for constables - 'Coppers', 'Crushers', 'Blue Bottles' or 'Peelers', liberally interspersed with profanities.

Shepherd thought back to his days down here with Beddows, and how by now, Beddows would have been across the road and treading on somebody's toes, literally, or sticking his finger up somebody's nostril. *'Not tonight,' he thought to himself, or rather 'Not yet, anyway!'*

As the two men approached the six old Almshouses that formed Cock Muck Hill, a larger group of men stood outside, one or two of whom looked to be holding pick axe handles, attempting to conceal them behind their backs, as the constables approached.

'Evening constables, what brings you two down here then? Not our normal wasters!' said a short fat man with receding hair, and a heavily pustuled, reddened face. The man smelled like a Slaughter-man, rancid and sweaty.

'And who wants to know, exactly?' said Shepherd.

'The Cock Muck Hill Defence Company, that's who!'

'Does Cock Muck Hill need a defence company then, my friend?' said Shepherd.

'We thinks it does, and that's what we're here for,' replied the spokesman.

'Well you can all go home now, because we are here, and that is what we are going to do,' said Shepherd.

'Not if you're like the other wasters that normally come down here. They'd be in the Mansfield Head by now, soaking it up in the back!' said the short, fat man, laughing cynically.

'Well they're gone, and my colleague and I are down here from now on. And, let it be known, things are going to be different,' said Shepherd.

'We'll believe that when we see it,' said someone at the back.

'And we start now. Clear off, and take your weapons with you. We don't want to see you again!' said Perkins, keen to make his mark.

'We'll leave when we're sure you've got it sorted. 'Til then, we stay,' said the spokesman.

'And what's your name then?' said Shepherd.

'Elijah Black. Porky to me mates!'

'Ah, and it was your Ma who got her window smashed the other night?' said Shepherd.

'That's right. Frightened the poor old dear half to death it did. And all while your mates were getting pissed in the Mansfield; them and their useless Sergeant!' said Porky.

'Well, we're not them, and our Sergeant is a good bloke too,' said Perkins, 'so bugger off and do as you're asked'.

'And what if we don't?' asked Porky.

Shepherd stepped forward and pressed his size eleven, hard into the well scuffed boot of Porky Black, grinding it, whilst he looked menacingly into the man's face. 'I had a good teacher, and I don't do being threatened. Last chance to go home, now, or else you'll see first-hand how we intend to sort things out from now on'.

'No need for that now, is there, Constable...?' said Porky.
'Constable Shepherd. And this is Constable Perkins.
Remember our names, and pass them around. You'll get
used to them soon enough.'

At that point, the group of men, with the exception of
Porky Black, walked dejectedly off towards Abbey
Street, the safety of the far side of Belgrave Gate, with
the prospect of warm beds, unlike Shepherd and
Perkins, for whom the night was young.

*'Not much of a defence company amongst the lot of them.
Very strong, but easily led – a bit like the sheep they no
doubt slaughter!'* thought Shepherd.

Porky Black stood outside his Ma's hovel, and said to the
constables 'We're all on your side, really, you know. We
only want to make sure these old uns don't come to no
harm,' grimacing as he reflected on the pain in his toes,
now slowly subsiding. 'That hurt me, Mr Shepherd.'

'To win this battle, we're going to do everything and
anything that gives us an edge. If you think standing on
someone's toes is going to be enough, then you're
mistaken. That was nothing to what we'll have to do, so
be warned, and be careful. We are the law. Make sure
that is the message that goes around!' said Shepherd.

'Don't suppose I could interest you in a cuppa?' said
Porky.

'Only a quickie and to say hello to your Ma!' said
Shepherd, smiling, easing the tension.

*****

The hovel was small, cramped and dark, as Shepherd
had suspected. There was only a rickety, well-worn
armchair, a crooked three-legged stool and a table that
had long seen better days. A grossly inadequate small
fire burned in the grate and a kettle hung from the spit

that hung across the embers. Shepherd doubted whether the spit had ever seen meat, but then again, he recognised that with a butcher for a son, she probably ate better than most in the other five hovels. A privvie slop bucket sat in one corner, foul smelling, not emptied for some days probably. Poor old soul couldn't get as far as the outside privvie in the communal yard, and probably safer not to. The bedroom would no doubt be similarly sad and shabby. The whole place smelled of stale urine, predominantly, as came with very old folk and their diminishing physical and mental well being. Both constables were quickly aware of the insect activity, and the room seemed to be infested with bugs, lice and large black beetles, crawling over every surface, the candle light catching on their scaly surfaces. *The old lady must be alive with them,' thought Shepherd.*

'These two constables are going to keep you safe, Ma,' said Porky, rinsing out four old jam jars, with chipped and crooked tops, and which had long seen better days! They had once been prized by his Father, who had brought them back from the Napoleonic wars, 'seized from Napoleon's own cooks', his Father had once told him. The rinsing water stood in an old ceramic bowl, and looked grey and murky in the candle-light.

Perkins looked decidedly green at the thought of what was to be offered.

'You'll drink out of worse than this by the time we've left the Rookeries,' whispered Shepherd, 'so now stop being a baby and watch me.'

Porky poured out four measures of the pale brown liquid, and then apologised as there was no milk left in the larder. 'I take it you'll have it without then?' smiled Porky, apologetically.

'So long as it's warm and wet,' said Shepherd, smiling reassuringly at the old lady. 'Now tell us what's been going on,' raising the jar to his lips but stopping just short, as he spoke.

Perkins watched him closely.

'The place gets visited every other day. Gangs of 'incomers'; all demanding money, and if they haven't got money, they help themselves to coal or the likes. Greedy, lazy bastards they are. The Micks were never like that. They keep themselves to themselves at the moment. Green Street has never been so quiet, but now this lot is picking on these poor old souls,' said Porky.

'We'll put a stop to that, before we do anything else,' said Shepherd, holding his tea to his chin.

'Where are these incomers coming from?' said Perkins.

'Rumour has it they're to do with one of them big lodging houses, like Abigail Hextall's, but down in Bateman's Yard, off Bateman's Row. Like a maze it is. They call this place *The Rats' Castle*, so word has it!' said Porky.

'Well, we all know what happens to rats in the end, don't we?' said Shepherd.

'So, they might be round again, tonight?' enquired Perkins.

'A bit late now,' said Porky. 'Probably on the grog by now, somewhere they feels safe, more like.'

'So we had better go and find them, in that case,' said Shepherd, slowly emptying the contents of the grubby jar down into the small slop bucket in the corner.

Perkins quickly followed suit. 'Thanks for the tea. We'll pop by from time to time if that's all right?'

Mrs Black nodded wearily, looking her age; shocked and vacant.

Porky opened the flimsy door for the two men to leave. 'You mind yourselves down here. These are a bad lot, and don't have any respect for any of the locals. All you need to do, is let me know, and I'll have our boys down here to back you up, drop of a hat!' said Porky.

'I hope your toes are alright now?' said Shepherd. 'I would have preferred not to do so, but I don't take kindly to challenges!'

'Point made, Mr Shepherd, point made. One of your old mates did that to me once when I'd had a pint or two, too many. Constable Beddows as I recall.'

'That doesn't surprise me,' said Shepherd, smiling.

'By the way; sorry about the glasses, Mr Perkins, but they're all she's got, and she's still very proud of them, them being Napoleon's own and all that. I don't think we will have poisoned you though, gave them a good wash first, so don't you worry.'

Chapter Three – 'Lines in the sand'

Leaving Cock Muck Hill, the two men walked left, and towards Abbey Street and Green Street, with their rough, entwined, yards and alleys that made up the predominantly Irish quarter.

This would be where, in days past, Shepherd would have expected the greatest resistance. However, the cramped and dingy streets were quieter than he had expected and apart from one or two small groups who looked menacing, stood at the entry to Hextall's 'Pork Shop' Yard and Dent's Yard, no doubt there to block any assault on their own strongholds. They would not venture far from their alleyways, and would not become a problem unless the constables decided to try their hand and gain entry.

The community here was close; very close. The Irish would be hunkering down in the filth, forming their own local ceili, drawing on their dudeens, shouting, singing and swearing, as the Irish did as norm. Many would be drunk, as they were most of the day, these days. The alleyways seemed alive around the clock. The men would be considering whether to stay and defend, or venture out and see off any threats.

These were not the 'Fancy' or the bruisers that filled the Irish pubs, who were now moving into Wharf Street and better housing, funded by their ill gotten gains of past years. These were the common Irish; the hawkers and chip-choppers, the mat and swag makers, the greenceens, not the chancers. All were hungry, with their diet of potato soup or stew, perhaps thickened with some bread or grain. Few had ever tasted meat. *Money spent on meat was money less for grog!*

A few of them were good, strong labourers, and many would be found in the day, putting finishing touches to the new 'Corn Exchange' in the Market Place, building of which had commenced the year before; an ornate, white painted, single level centre-piece for the 'new look' Borough, and much admired and promoted by Mayor Dove Harris and his Aldermen.

These skilled men would no doubt move out of the Rookeries as soon as they could afford better.

It had been venturing out onto Mansfield Street and Sandacre Street lately, and having their heads broken and arses kicked, that had led the current Irish community to conclude that they were no longer 'top dogs' and thus, needed to review their position, and withdraw to their alleyways.

A few loud jeers followed the constables, but no physical challenge.

'This just isn't right,' said Shepherd. 'This is not like the Irish of old.'

Wandering round by the end of Abbey Street, they stopped at the junction with Belgrave Gate, as they were due a 'point' at ten forty-five with Sergeant Wright. Shepherd's fob watch showed him that they were pushing it, and would get it in the neck, if they weren't there as detailed.

As they crossed over the street and reached the corner, Sergeant Wright appeared in view, walking slowly and upright, down Haymarket, and towards them, splitting groups of men and women outside the gin palaces that lit up most of Haymarket and Belgrave Gate; swinging his truncheon, casually but menacingly, as he strolled along at regulation pace, occasionally pausing to rebuke some drunk or loudmouth.

'You two have not made much of an impression, yet then?' said Sergeant Wright.

'Why's that, Sergeant?' said Shepherd.

'You're both still upright and walking about. I take it our Irish friends haven't given you your obligatory kicking as of yet. Or have they seen you off already?' Wright smiled.

'Our Irish friends are definitely not themselves at the moment,' said Shepherd. 'It looks very *territorial*, at present. Each gang has got men on the entries to their own yards and mazes, but there's nobody roaming. Mind, it is early yet. Once the pubs tip out we'll probably regret it.'

'Right then, I understand that Mr Charters wants you to be flexible, so I don't want another point until one fifteen, just so as I know you are both still alive,' said Wright.

'Thanks Sarge,' said Shepherd. 'We won't let anyone down'.

'You keep an eye on his back Constable Perkins. And no going off being too bleeding cocky and starting something you can't finish!' said Wright.

'You can trust me to look after Constable Shepherd, Sergeant. Mind, he seems to have a bit of edge down here already!'

*****

The two men walked slowly up Belgrave Gate, across Abbey Street, right, into Baker Street and back towards Cock Muck Hill. The rumours had suggested that the protagonists in all the current trouble were 'incomers' who had a stronghold in Sandacre Street, therefore, it was time to do some 'noseying' around down there. The sky was quite light, looking North-West, and above the three story dwellings at the end of the street that formed Bateman's Yard and Bateman's Row, the tower of St Margaret's Church appeared to cast a wary frown over the melancholy housing and their melancholy occupants.

Looking down towards Bateman's Row, the constables could see that there was a large group of men and women stood outside the front of The Mansfield Head, which still looked to be open and serving; not a good sign. The group was also growing in number with every pace the constables took, as more people spilled outside at news of their approach.

The group began to move across the road, forming a human barrier, all facing the approaching threat of the Law.

'Looks like they don't want us here,' said Perkins.

'Looks that way to me, just be careful. No heroics and no stupidity, understand?' said Shepherd.

'And to what do we owe the pleasure of Crushers down in our neck of the woods?' said a large built male, moving to the front of the assembled group.

The man's accent suggested to Shepherd that he was a southerner, probably from around the London area, as he had heard one before and it sounded familiar. A fair number were known to have moved up when the St Giles Rookeries over-flowed, in search of foundry work.

'This is now our beat, so we will be down here regularly, and we intend to make sure that you are all kept safe and well, given the current troubles,' said Shepherd.

'Well you can just turn round and bugger off. We don't need Crushers hanging around down here, we look after it ourselves. God help anyone who thinks different. Your other mates don't bother us, so bugger off!' said the spokesman.

'Well that might be how it was, but as of today the two of us are going to be down here; morning, noon and night; us, not our mates,' said Perkins.

'Does your daddy know you're out this late, sonny Jim?' said a woman in the group, causing spontaneous laughter and cheers to break out amongst the group.

'At least I know who my daddy is, which is probably more than most of you lot,' quipped Perkins.

'Cocky little bugger, I'll knock your block off!' said the large Londoner, stepping forward, followed by two or three rough looking men dressed in open waistcoats, scruffy shirts and vests and scuffed boots. Most of the men looked the worse for drink.

'Leave it, Jim. We don't need grief from this lot as well,' called a voice from the back; a man who looked vaguely familiar to Shepherd.

'There'll be no violence from any of you, else it will be a trip to the Gaol for anyone who crosses the line,' said Shepherd, stepping in front of Perkins.

'And you think you'll stop me?' said the man now identified as 'Jim'.

'I think I will try,' said Shepherd, slowly coiling the strap of his truncheon around his wrist and fist, not taking his eyes off the men at the front of the group. Out of the corner of his eye, he noted Perkins making similar movements.

'I'll have both of you for me supper,' the man continued. Two of the men along side of 'Jim' started to move out, as if to out-flank the constables, at which point Shepherd felt Perkins move slightly behind him. They had a good fighting position, at present.

'If anyone comes a step closer, you shall feel the full weight of my truncheon,' shouted Shepherd, his voice raised in pitch as his body prepared itself for a fight. Shepherd's stick came into view and he held it out in front of him, reinforcing his threat. Perkins' was also visible to his side.

'Get them, lads!' the man 'Jim' called out, moving more quickly now and filling the gap that offered the constables a little time, at least, to react.

The threat of at least three men was enough to give Shepherd justification to use his truncheon. This would be its 'christening' on a human being, as he had only used it once before - to kill an injured, but vicious, dog. He briefly recalled his anxiety, when he first joined, as to whether it would sound and feel like the 'priest' he used to kill Salmon, back on the Trent at home in Nottingham. But he knew he didn't have that much time to think, and reacted instinctively.

Shepherd brought the length of hard wood, purposefully down and across the advancing man's right shoulder. There was a squeal, and a dull 'tank' as the wood struck bone, and then bounced off, striking the man's right cheek on rebound. Shepherd briefly recalled why Tanky Smith allegedly got his nickname. The man dropped to his knees, in clear pain, before trying to regain his composure and resume his attack.

'I wouldn't try again, if I were you,' said Shepherd. 'That was a warning; the next one will be in earnest!'

The men in the group began to spread out, and Shepherd suspected that they were now going to have to be even more resolute.

'Mind yourself, Perkins. These beggars are not backing off.'

Perkins was already eyeing up his first 'victim', should they progress any nearer.

'Come on then, who's next?' shouted Perkins, anger now raging, and not at all, apparently, afraid.

The original spokesman 'Jim', was now supported by a very loud, drunken woman, who appeared to be his 'trouble and strife' according to the taunting from the crowd – whatever that meant!

'Look what you've done to my old man; there was no need for that, I'll have you done for that,' she bellowed venomously, spitting at the two constables.

'Teach them a lesson lads; one that they'll not forget,' called out the drunken woman. Perkins noted she was heavily tattooed on her arms and around her neck. *'Ugly cow!' he thought.*

At her instigation, several of the men who had started to move around the constables, rushed forward.

Perkins struck out, hard and fast with his own truncheon, catching an advancing man across his shoulder and collar bone, just as they had been originally taught. The man seemed somewhat tougher and continued his attack, raising his fists and snarling; his eyes seeming to shine red, matching the colour of his face, well fuelled by grog, no doubt.

Perkins struck the man again, much harder, downwards across the middle of his forehead. The man seemed to stand upright, briefly, before falling forward and in a pile at Perkins' feet.

'That'll teach you, my old mate,' muttered Perkins, shaking his head. 'I'm going home tonight; whatever you lot may think to the contrary!'

Two men ran at Shepherd. He swung his truncheon, forcefully and at shoulder height, straight across the faces of the oncoming men, striking both and splashing blood over his colleague in the process. Both men stopped, momentarily, one falling to his knees. The other however, resumed his determined attack almost immediately, fuelled by drink, Shepherd suspected. Shepherd was not far enough back to get a further blow in, so instinctively he brought up his right foot in a sweeping upward kick, catching the man hard in the 'crown jewels'. The man joined his mate on the floor.

Out of the gloom, a glint of something shiny and metallic momentarily caught Shepherd's eye, just as a cold, sharp blade connected with his left ear, slicing across the top of it and into his left cheek. He realised he had just been 'cut', but he did not know how badly. At this precise moment he did not care. He was still fit to fight.

'Perkins, a blade, mind out!' called Shepherd, as a man in a grey, sweaty vest came into better view, slashing wildly backwards and forwards across in front of him, with what appeared to be a cut-throat razor.

'Bastard Coppers. I'll show you what you get down here,' called out the man, planting both feet firmly down in front of the two constables in a gesture of defiance. Shepherd backed off a step, pulling Perkins back with his free hand, his truncheon held out in front of them both.

'You're hurt Shepherd, are you okay?'

'I'll be fine, just watch out.'

'This one's mine, Shepherd,' said Perkins, leaping forward, truncheon in hand, catching the man with the razor unprepared. Perkins brought his truncheon down brutally across the man's wrist, smashing the razor free from the man's grip. The sound of breaking bone seemed to fill the narrow street, even over the sound of the men fighting, and the baying crowd behind them, then a long, agonizing scream.

Perkins looked at the man - his face now only about a foot away, then promptly and viciously brought his forehead downward, head-butting the man and obliterating his nose, which bleed profusely, before he too fell to the floor.

'Bet you weren't taught that in the Police,' said Shepherd.

Shepherd quickly reached down and grabbed the handle of the open blade, removing it from temptation of others that were considering picking it up.

'Enough! We don't want anyone else getting hurt...so back off!' bellowed Shepherd.

Perkins regained his place, slightly to the side and slightly behind Shepherd. The men resumed their best fighting stance, yet again. Perkins was grinning wildly, wide eyed, totally enjoying the fight.

On the floor in front of them sat, or lay, a variety of prisoners and casualties. The original spokesman - the Londoner, Jim Gardener, now nursing what appeared to be a broken shoulder or arm; the two men who had first attacked Shepherd, Obadiah Woods and Dick Smythe, with their bloodied faces, one now with a particularly high voice; Perkins' first attacker, John Greenwood; and finally, the man now known to be Matthew Fletcher, who had originally been very brave with the razor, who clearly had a painful and badly broken arm and nose.

'Not bad for a few moments scrapping?' said Perkins, grinning. 'Mind you, you need to find your ear, 'cos half of it seems to be missing, as are our hats. Can't go back without them, can we?'

The two constables' headwear had vanished into the crowd and no doubt would be seen as trophies, albeit of a bitter defeat at the hands of the Law.

'Not a bad first show, Perkins. Now then, let's get some help,' said Shepherd, feeling for his ear, and realizing that the top of it was no longer there. Shepherd swung his rattle, as hard as he could, as his breath began to return and the adrenaline settled.

The crowd moved back and realised that this battle was over, but the war would go on.

'Next time, try us at the Rats' Castle,' came a cry from the group. 'Then we'll see how hard you really are.'

'That's really scary, coming from a group who are leaving their mates to go to prison. Not got a fight left among you?' shouted Perkins.

The sound of hob-nails on cobbles began to fill the air as, reluctantly, and eventually, one or two of their Colleagues responded to their assistance. Others, not brave enough to venture into the Rookeries, went off in the opposite direction.

Sergeant Wright was one of the first to arrive, out of breath; Topper in one hand and truncheon in the other. He surveyed the small group of injured men, and then looked across at Shepherd and Perkins.

'What did I say to you, not half an hour ago? I leave you alone and look what you get yourselves into!' Wright smiled, wryly. 'You alright Shepherd? Looks like you've lost half your ear.'

'That chap, there, seemed to think he could slice us up, and took it off with his razor,' said a chirpy Perkins, pointing out the relevant prisoner.

'In that case, we'd better secure this motley lot, and get them back to the Station,' said Wright. 'Constables Williams and Bradley, you keep an eye on this place for the next few hours. I think Constables Shepherd and Perkins will be rather busy!'

'By the way Shepherd, I think this might belong to you?' said Perkins, picking up the remnants of an ear from the dust and filth of the road. 'Know anyone that's good with a needle and thread?'

Chapter Four – 'A turn for the worse'

Shortly after midnight, back at Town Hall Lane, Shepherd and Perkins were sorting out the men they had earlier arrested. Shepherd also sought the attention of his friend, Tom Hamilton, the Surgeon, to do whatever he could with the remnants of his ear.

At about the same time, a disturbance broke out again, at the alms houses in Cock Muck Hill.

Sergeant Wright and several members of Shepherd's shift responded.

Upon his arrival, Sergeant Wright was met by a small group of terrified old folk; five in total. They were dressed in their day to day rags and one or two were crying and shaking, whilst urgently trying to tell the constables what had happened.

The only occupant not present was Aggie Black. The door to her hovel was splintered and wide open, as were all the others. Each had been kicked in by a gang of men a few minutes earlier, demanding coal and any coins or valuables the old folk may have had.

Sergeant Wright, with only his small Bulls-eye oil lamp for illumination, entered the small ground floor room. He could see that it was empty. Not a recogniseable stick of furniture was left in one piece. The floor was littered with the debris, broken wood and glass, which included the cherished jars from Napoleon's cook.

'Mrs Black, are you there?' called out Sergeant Wright, but there was no reply.

Slowly walking up the short and narrow stairs, which creaked and groaned under his weight, he entered the first floor bedroom, still illuminated with a stub of candle, giving a pale, eerie light.

Lying on the bed, facing upwards towards the sagging ceiling, eyes wide open, was the body of Aggie Black. The room appeared undisturbed, but Aggie's face was locked in a fearful gaze, a look of terror, her mouth open and toothless, as when gasping for her last breath. There were, otherwise, no signs of violence and her clothing appeared undisturbed, but Wright was confident that she was dead. Corpses have that certain look and feel about them. *'Never liked them'*, he thought quietly to himself. He had seen his fair share. She was icy cold to his touch.

Shutting the door to the bedroom, quickly, behind him, Sergeant Wright went back down to the small yard and ushered the constables to get the old people back into their own homes, advising them to remain inside for the time being.

'Constable Billson, go back to the Station. I want a detective sergeant down here, right away. Ask Sergeant Sheffield to advise Mr Goodyer that we have a dead body in Cock Muck Hill. We will also need a police surgeon,' said Wright, sending the constable post-haste, from the yard.

'You men,' he said, addressing the other constables now at the location. 'I want to know what each of these old folk saw and heard. Who were the people who did this? Get as much detail as you can, especially if anyone was known to them.'

*****

Constable Billson arrived at the Station, red faced and breathless. Inside the building, Sergeant Sheffield stood talking with Detective Sergeant Beddows; the prisoners were all locked up in the cells and Perkins and Shepherd sat in the scullery, where Surgeon Thomas Hamilton was sewing together Shepherd's ear, looking very adept with needle, sewing thread, and a bowl of boiling hot water.

'Can't be too careful, need to keep that clean,' said Hamilton. 'It'll hurt like buggery for a few days; then I'll take the thread out for you. It will make you look very distinguished, but a bit lop-sided.'

'Thanks, Tom,' said Shepherd, wincing as Hamilton tied a final delicate knot.

'What's up with you, Constable Billson?' asked a grumpy Sergeant Sheffield.

'There's a dead body down in Cock Muck Hill. Sergeant Wright wants a detective, a surgeon and Mr Charters to be informed,' said Billson, now short of breath and clearly unfit.

'I thought constables were supposed to be healthy specimens? Too much ale and not enough walking about!' said a bemused Beddows. 'We'd better go and break the good news to Mr Charters. Mr Hamilton; I wouldn't leave just yet, as I suspect we may shortly need your skills again.'

Beddows and Billson walked across the yard from the rear door of the Station, and to the front door of Mr Charters' house, within the confines of Town Hall yard. A light was still burning in one of the ground-floor front rooms. Mr Charters quickly came to the door, still dressed in his uniform.

'What is it, Beddows?' said Charters.

'We've had a disturbance in Cock Muck Hill, and Sergeant Wright has found a body. He wants a detective and a surgeon and that we should inform you of the facts, sir.'

'I thought Shepherd and Perkins were down there. What are they doing?' said Charters.

'They were, sir, but in a confrontation, Shepherd had part of his ear cut off. They've arrested five prisoners already, all of whom are currently locked up across the yard. This happened after they had left with their prisoners, by the sound of it,' said Beddows.

'Right; I'll just get my cap and then we'd best be off. Who is the police surgeon tonight?' said Charters.

'Mr Hamilton is in the Station sewing up Shepherd's ear, as we speak.'

'Well, I will need him to come with us,' said Charters, as the three men walked back across the yard and into the Station.

*****

'Can't I leave you to do a simple task without it raining dead bodies?' said Charters, looking across at Shepherd and Perkins with astonishment.

'Sounds like it's all broken out after we left, sir,' said Shepherd. 'The prisoners are from outside the Mansfield Head. We had left Cock Muck Hill, quite some time earlier.'

'I bet there's a connection though,' said Charters. 'I suppose we'd better go and see what we've got. Mr Hamilton, have you finished with Shepherd?'

'Yes, but unfortunately I couldn't sew his ear back together, so he'll look a bit lop-sided for the rest of his service,' said Hamilton, smiling broadly.

'Do what you have to do with your prisoners. Sergeant Sheffield, throw the book at them. Every charge you can put together. I'm not having my men carved like one of Mr Keetley's roasts, across the road!' barked Charters, as the four men left the building.

Sergeant Sheffield drew on his pipe, the aromatic smoke filling his lungs, closed his eyes and nodded politely.

*****

Sergeant Wright led the three men upstairs to Aggie Black's Spartan bedroom. He had sourced some further oil lamps, and the light was now sufficient to see much more and to offer Tom Hamilton enough light to make a preliminary examination of the body.

'No signs of physical violence?' said Charters.

'Only to the hovel itself,' said Beddows.

'Who decided she was dead?' said an irate Hamilton.

'I did,' said Wright. 'Why?'

'This woman's still alive. Her pulse is very weak. I think she has had some sort of an episode, which has affected her heart. We need to get her to the Infirmary, and quickly,' said Hamilton.

'Sergeant; go and hail a cab!' Charters barked at Sergeant Wright.

'Didn't anyone tell you, always make sure they're dead?' Beddows muttered, shaking his head. He cast his mind back to the lesson he had taught Shepherd, back on the riverbank the year previous, and his favourite tale of a young and experienced physician, a decomposing body and the search for a long departed pulse.

'That's the trouble with you uniformed boys; never make a detective to save your own life, let alone anyone else's.'

'Sod off, Beddows. It's a mistake anyone could have made,' mumbled Wright, visibly reddening around the face.

'I need some bellows and some tobacco,' said Hamilton.

'Whatever for man?' said Charters.

'We need to blow tobacco smoke through her rectum and into her guts. There is a suggestion that this irritant effect may cause a reaction when people are in this state,' said Hamilton. 'I've seen it done, once before.'

'I've heard some strange things in my time. Let me try and get hold of some bellows,' said Beddows, disappearing down the stairs, shaking his head.

Within moments, Beddows returned, bellows in hand. 'I've got a pipe, what do I do next?'

'Light it man, quickly now,' said Hamilton.

Once the pipe was alight, Hamilton used the bellows and drew in the acrid smoke, having already turned the old lady over, in a very undignified and rushed manner, and exposed her naked rump to the small group of men.

He abruptly inserted the tip of the bellows into Aggie Black's rectum, and forcefully closed the handles of the bellows, thrusting the smoke, deep, inside her body.

'And again please,' said Hamilton.

'What?' said Beddows. 'You want to stick that bit that's just been up her arse, back into the bowl of my favourite pipe?'

'Just get on with it, Beddows, you old woman,' said Charters.

Hamilton quickly repeated the bizarre procedure when, shockingly, there was a groan from the old lady, and her eyes rolled and her mouth slowly moved, followed by a loud, rasping fart, as the poor old dear expelled the excess wind and smoke.

'Now I've seen everything,' said Beddows. 'I knew my old lady could talk out of her arse, but that beggars belief.'

'Cab's here, sir,' called Constable Billson from downstairs.

'Right; let's get her off to the Infirmary,' said Hamilton, grabbing his case.

'What about my pipe?' said Beddows.

'Smells like shit that you're smoking most of the time anyway, man,' said Charters, in his broadest Geordie accent. 'Sergeant Wright, I want you to go with the good Doctor and Mrs Black, and stay with her; she might still help us yet. Sergeant Beddows, I want you to speak with the constables and the other residents and find out who is behind this. I am going back to the Station. Keep me updated with any news.'

'Yes sir. What about arrests?' said Beddows.

'Come back in first, unless you have no other choice. I want to see what and who we are dealing with. In the meantime, as far as anyone is concerned, the old lady is dead, understand?' said Charters, with a knowing, devious look.

'I think I'm with you, sir,' said Beddows

Chapter Five – 'The Rats' Castle'

'What a bastard waste of time that was,' shouted Edward Cox, the newly self-announced leader of the Rats' Castle mob. 'Old bastards didn't have nothing worth pinching – yet again! Any of you get anything from your endeavours?'

The small group of men entered via a filth-ridden, flimsy door, in the corner of the main room of the gloomy lodging house, located at the far end of Bateman's Yard, and down a winding dark alleyway.

The room had been laid out in the style of a small hostelry, and Jenny Harper, the wife of the Lodging House owner, Francis Harper, was busily pouring out large measures of cheap gin, and passing them to other women in the room to ferry over to Cox and his cohorts. Leicester had about 38 such lodging houses at this time, and about six hundred transients used them, night after night. Many were of a similar nature to the one in Bateman's Yard, with illegal bars, but few were gang strongholds, Pork Shop Yard perhaps having the nearest alike, but that was within the Irish quarter.

A few miserable, bedraggled men and women already sat around tables in the dark room, drinking and playing cards; children scurrying or sitting around at their feet, as Cox and his gang walked back in. Not everyone had been involved in tonight's foray. A mix of pick-pockets and Burglars mainly, or con artists of some description, their own, unique, evening's work done, had been back for some time, and handed over their ill gotten gains to one or two of the local 'fences' who were allowed access for long enough to trade.

'Old buggers had nothing. Just a few old rings and some medals was all they had between them. Their coal has run out and they are due some more this next week, one of them told me, so we picked the wrong night,' said Fred Bell, another Londoner, who had come to Leicester in the last few months and was on the run from the Police in Bow. 'Don't know why we didn't do the Micks down Green Street. At least we'd have got grog and baccy!'

'It weren't the wrong night. If I said it was the right night, it was the right night,' said Cox, banging his empty glass down hard on the table, before stretching out for another, squeezing the passing girl's immature breasts, having a good old grope, for good measure.

'Fat tart,' he spat, looking at the plump girl, who also happened to be his youngest daughter. 'About time you got wed, buggered off and saved me some coin. You're nearly thirteen and should be hitched by now, with a couple of sprogs, like your mother was. Anyway Fred, we don't need to push our luck with the Micks, as we are short of a bit of muscle after the skirmish at the old Mansfield!'

'That's no way to treat a kid,' said 'Sailor' Brooks, who had come back in with the other odds and sods from his personal thieving endeavours, much earlier.

'Who the hell d'you think you are? You've been with us five minutes and you start telling me what to do. D'you want a good hiding too? Mind your own bleeding business and just do your job if you want to stay in my company,' bellowed Cox.

'Didn't mean to offend,' said the bearded newcomer. 'I've just seen too many young girls taken advantage of, lately. The old Navy boys treat them awful, and they ain't old enough or big enough to stand up for themselves.'

'Didn't think sailors had any problem shagging anyone; boys or girls, know what I mean?' said Cox, swigging hard on his gin.

'We got a problem, Coxy,' said one of the other men at Cox's table; a Welshman named Phillips, an ex Guardsman from Cardiff, who had married a Leicester girl in Pembroke Dock, and come back to Leicester with her and the false promise of some labouring work.

'And prey, why do we have a problem? Do *you* mean *you* have a problem, *we* have a problem, or *I* have a problem?' said Cox.

'All of them, I think,' said Phillips. 'One of the old ladies opened her door, upstairs, whilst I was searching her hovel. I went up to shut her up, but she was lying on her bed, eyes open, see. I think she dropped down dead on me.'

'You fucking idiot. I said they were old and to go easy, not to fucking kill one of them!' bellowed Cox. 'Did anyone down there know you?'

'Only you lot know me. Bella and me keep ourselves to ourselves, even during the day. Never been into any of them houses before, honest; one or two in Green Street, but never in Cock Muck Hill.'

'Got anything of hers that'll hang you, if you get caught with it?' said Cox.

'Weren't nothing worth pinching. Furniture was falling to bits, and I might have helped it along a bit, but nothing. No coin, no coal, no rings; nothing! Must have scared her to death, though,' said Phillips.

'Well, just keep your big Welsh gob shut. Bleedin' hell, what about the rest of you? Anything you've got needs moving on and damned quick, too. Where's Isaac the Jew? He'll have to get rid of it for us, quick,' said a worried Cox.

'Gone to his brother's in Applegate Street,' said Brooks. 'Least I think that's what he said. He was shifting some trinkets for me, if you know what I mean.'

'Well go and find the little shit. I want him back here, and quick, else I'll have your trinkets, if you know what I mean?' said Cox.

Brooks left the table and went out into the alleyway that led out onto Bateman's Row and Sandacre Street, passing pairs of Cox's men who were there as enforcers. Nobody would get in to the Rats' Castle, not without going mob handed.

What made it even riskier, was that mingling in with the gang members were large numbers of women and young children, babes in arms, and the normal array of mangy cats and dogs, sitting or lying amongst the litter and debris abandoned by the hapless residents. The lodging house was almost behind barricades made up of assorted humans and their waste. Ironically, the alleys were also the home of large, black rats, which scurried around, chased by the cats and the kids, a fitting addition to the Castle's reputation.

'Where are you off then, Brooksy?' said one of the men at the front entrance to the yard.

'Got to find Isaac the Jew, for Cox,' said Brooks. 'Any ideas?'

'Applegate Street, counting his money I would think,' the man laughed.

'Just what I thought too,' said Brooks, scurrying off, head down, collar up.

*****

Sailor Brooks took a brisk walk, up Churchgate, through Eastgates and up High Street, heading for the narrow

three story house on Applegate Street, where he hoped
he would find Isaac the Jew.

The streets were still busy, and he got a long stare from
a couple of constables along the route, and fearing he
was going to be stopped and searched, he pulled his
collar up higher, tucked his head down and increased
his pace. *'Not tonight,' he thought to himself, 'not tonight,
please!'*

Nobody called out, and he passed by, safely, arriving at
the house about three or four minutes later.

The clock on St Nicholas church struck quarter to two,
as the faded door, with its flaking paint and dirty bevels
was opened, cautiously.

Isaac the Jew looked around carefully, before loosening
a chain and allowing Brooks inside.

'You sure you weren't followed?' said Isaac.

'Nearly got stopped by a couple of nosey constables on
High Street, but no, definitely not, otherwise,' said
Brooks.

'Better shut the bleedin door then,' said Isaac, closing
the night out.

'We need to speak. Cox wants you, urgently!' said
Brooks.

*****

Beddows was just starting to talk to the last of the
remaining old folk, when he became aware of shouting
from out on Mansfield Street. It was evident that there
were a growing number of raised voices.

Leaving the old lady sitting talking with Constable
Billson, Beddows went out and was confronted by a
group of about ten men, all armed with pickaxe handles,
and at the front of the group stood Porky Black, red
faced, as usual, but sobbing loudly.

'They've killed my old ma, and you bastards have let them,' screamed Porky. 'Told you that you should have left it to us, but no, you lot were supposed to look after her.'

'Porky, we need to speak. All of you come into the yard with me now, it's important.'

'Come with you?' screamed Porky. 'We're going to find whoever done this and bring them to justice ourselves.' For the second time in not so many hours, Porky Black winced as Beddows brought his heavy soled heel down across his toes, and ground it in to Porky's toes. 'Don't ever threaten me you short-arse, fat little shit bag - ever again; even if you're upset. Just bleeding listen to me for a minute.'

'What then?' shouted Porky, spittle flying from his lips onto Beddows' face, which Beddows wiped away instantly, with the sleeve of his jacket.

'You need to go to the Infirmary. Ask for Sergeant Wright, and if I was you, I'd make my way there pronto. I'm saying no more than that. Sergeant Wright will explain everything to you when you get there.'

'I want to see what they've done to her home,' said Porky.

'You can do that later. Right now, I would suggest you would far sooner be at the Infirmary, believe me,' said Beddows. 'I can't tell you anything more than that, but trust me.'

'What about whoever's done this?' screamed Porky.

'We are starting to get statements about what went on. Constable Shepherd has five prisoners from an earlier disturbance, and we have more information that is now making sense. We will sort this out, not you and your mob,' said Beddows.

'Is it the bleeding Irish, or those bleeders from Sandacre Street?' said Porky.

'I'm not saying yet. I want to be sure before we jump to conclusions,' said Beddows. 'Get down to the Infirmary, seriously, and don't hang around. If I was you I'd dump your weapons and I'd go up Baker Street and get straight off the Rookeries to get there. We don't need any more trouble tonight. If I see any one of you with a weapon down here again, I'll arrest the lot of you, and you'll wish you hadn't been born by the time I finish with you. I don't give many second chances,' said Beddows.

It was quite clear to the assembled men that Beddows was serious, and the other uniformed constables who were gathered, began to usher the men away.

'Steer clear of Abbey Street or Green Street tonight, as the Irish are all sat waiting. Baker Street is the best way out of here tonight, I shalln't tell you again,' said Beddows. 'Leave your weapons inside your ma's front door; they'll be safe there tonight.'

'Who's coming with me to the Infirmary?' said Porky.

The group left as one man, following in Porky's wake.

Chapter Six – 'A mischief of rats'

Sailor Brooks and Isaac the Jew made their way, independently, back to Bateman's Yard and the lair of the Rats' Castle, arriving sometime after half past two. Both were wary of Cox's wrath, had they loitered unnecessarily, and apart from a brief stop for Isaac the Jew, to drop off some of the earlier contraband on the way back down, they were both sitting in the main room by quarter to three.

'Where the fuck have you two been?' demanded Cox.

'The constables are out in force tonight, and we had to be careful getting back. Loads of the perishers around on Mansfield Street, and I had to come through the alleys to avoid them,' said Brooks.

'What about you?' said Cox, staring harshly at Isaac the Jew.

The man's large hooked nose twitched, uncomfortably and he shrugged his shoulders. 'I didn't want to get stopped, not with tonight's takings, so I dropped them off on the way round. Safe now, they are. No doubt there will be a few coins for everyone by the morning,' Isaac replied. He pulled his black brimmed hat low, and seemed to shrink into his grubby black morning coat that he had taken a shine to from earlier proceeds of crime. His fingers pulled at his beard, nervously.

'A bit keen to get rid tonight, aren't we?' said Cox.

'Sailor told me there had been a bit of a problem, so I thought it best,' replied the Jew.

'Well we've got some more pressing 'takings' to get rid of, and you would have done better to have waited and took them all together; Would have got a better price wouldn't you?' Cox barked.

'Don't you worry about the price or getting rid, my dear,' said the Jew. 'I am confident that I can get you the best price in Leicester. When have I ever let you down before?'

'This lot is red hot; dangerous; and it could get us all hung. Get rid and get rid quick, and out of Leicester - if you have any sense, old man,' said Cox, handing Isaac a small bundle with every last bit of contraband from the Cock Muck Hill hovels.

'These medals are definitely too hot for Leicester, my dear; they have someone's name on, whoever Ghuznee is?' said Isaac, looking obliviously stupid.

'You silly old fucker,' growled Cox. 'Ghuznee was a battle. It's not someone's name, but it shows it belongs to someone who fought there, that's why it's dangerous to get rid of it here!'

'Why not just throw it away, and be done with it?' asked Fred Bell.

'And have taken the risk for nothing? No, sell it!' said Cox.

'What about London? Have you got any old contacts down there?' said Brooks.

'Why London? It doesn't need to go that far. Anyway, I'm sure Isaac the Jew has more contacts in London than do I,' said Cox.

'Just thought it might be safer,' said Brooks, trying to be helpful.

'Cost more to get there, than all the stuff's worth altogether,' said Cox. 'What about Birmingham? That's safer and much nearer. You can be there and back in a day or two?' said Cox.

'I have a cousin in Small Heath. He'll know who will have it from us, but it may delay getting a payment,' said the Jew.

'Well you pay me as soon as you've sold it,' said Cox. 'Just get rid of it, and quick. I want it out of Leicester tonight!'

'I'll see you gentlemen in a day or two then?' said the Jew.

'And don't try and do a runner, cos I'll find you, and I'll cut your ugly great nose off if you try anything to cross me. Two days at the most, understand? And if I ain't here, ask in the Mansfield; the Landlord will know how to get hold of me,' said Cox.

'Sounds like you're doing a runner, Mr Cox?' said the Jew.

'If Phillips has fucked things up for us all, we'll all need to run!' snarled Cox, glaring at the incompetent Welshman.

'D'you want me to go with him, keep an eye on him?' said Brooks.

'Good idea, make sure he gets it sorted,' said Cox. 'Any mischief, and teach him a lesson he'll not forget, fence or not. Then you can bring me the money!'

'Meet me back at Applegate Street later. We'll get the early coach to Birmingham,' said the Jew, looking across to Sailor Brooks.

'Too obvious,' said Brooks. 'The constables will be watching the stage coaches, they always do. They know who comes and who goes, so not a good idea. I know a bloke with a horse or two and a cart; he delivers to Birmingham every other day, so we might be lucky.'

'Good idea,' said Cox. 'Just get it sorted.'

*****

At eight o'clock on the morning of Tuesday the 4th of March, 1851, gathered in the house of Head Constable Charters were Mr Charters himself, Detective Sergeants

Beddows, Smith, Haynes, Kettle and Constables
Shepherd and Perkins.

'How's the ear?' said Beddows.

'Rather sore at present,' said Shepherd.

'Nice stitching!' said Perkins. 'I'll have to ask Mr
Hamilton to do my socks when they next need darning.'

'And the prisoners are all charged?' ask Charters

'All are charged with Breach of the peace; All are
charged with assaulting Perkins and myself, as
constables while in the execution of our duty; Matthew
Fletcher is charged with unlawfully and maliciously
cutting and wounding me. Will all be up before Mr
Hildyard this morning,' said Shepherd.

'So, four will go down for a month or two with hard
labour, but only one will get a lifetime trip to the
Colonies, more's the pity,' said Beddows, shaking his
head.

'Enough banter,' said Charters. 'Those charges will stop
and make people think for a while. News from the
Infirmary is that Mrs Black is alive; just! However, she
can presently remember nothing, whatsoever, of the
incident.'

'Don't think that's a problem now, sir,' said Tanky Smith.
'Black Tommy and me have first rate information as to
who has done it, as you are now aware, and we know
where the property is that was taken, and all who was
involved.'

'We have good descriptions from the old folk at Cock
Muck Hill, and they say that the men were not locals,
and that one at least was Welsh,' said Beddows.

'That fits in with our information. A Welsh bloke called
Phillips is the one who personally did old Ma Black's
abode. Do we know who, if anyone, had medals taken?'
said Black Tommy.

'Nobody mentioned any missing medals, from what's been said. Probably need another visit when they feel more up to it. Porky Black's dad was in the 'Leicestershires' and was killed in Afghanistan. He would have had service medals I suppose. Mind, many of the widows are probably the same and some of the blokes might even have served themselves, poor old buggers,' said Beddows.

'How have you got this information so quickly?' said Perkins, inquisitively.

'What Tommy and I do is for us to know,' said Tanky. 'Suffice to say we have men on the inside now, and they are quite reliable. They even got all of the property back for us.'

'What would we do without you two?' asked Shepherd. Smith moved his lips but no words could be heard.

'What was that?' said Shepherd.

Smith moved his lips again, but nothing could be heard.

'Sorry, I can't hear you...' said Shepherd.

'It's probably something to do with only having half an ear?' Smith laughed.

'Ha-ha; very good,' said Shepherd, realising his stupidity.

'We'll have to call you Arfur from now on,' said Black Tommy, 'as our little term of endearment.'

'Arfur?' said Shepherd.

'As in only having half a ear,' said Black Tommy, also now laughing, with tears rolling down his cheeks.

'You walked into that one, Shepherd,' said Charters.

'I'm walking into far too much these days, jokes and all,' said Shepherd. 'I need to sharpen my reactions to a lot of things.'

'The gang members that are responsible for Cock Muck Hill are getting twitchy. They've sent two of their own off to Birmingham, supposedly, to fence the jewellery and medals that were stolen from the six houses. They're worried because they think Mrs Black is dead, and they'll get necked for their endeavours,' said Charters.

'Do you think they're going to do a runner?' said Beddows.

'We can't rule that out, so I want someone to hang around near Sandacre Street, and watch for any strange movement. Make sure nobody leaves there and gets on a coach today,' said Charters.

'Why can't we just go down mob handed and arrest them all, sir?' asked Perkins.

'Too many women and kids about, and the place is a veritable fortress, from what we have been told. We need to get them when they go out on their little capers, so tonight we stand a better chance; catch them on our terms!'

'Observations would normally be a job for Tommy and me?' said Tanky Smith. 'Could do with a couple of hours kip though; been a long night.'

'You should have been down there with us; that was really a rough night,' said Perkins.

'What do you think we do all night, son?' asked Black Tommy, abruptly.

'Let us just say Sergeants Smith and Haynes have had a fruitful night, and we are indebted to them, again,' said Charters. 'What I want then is you Kettle, to start off the observations. Find somewhere safe and don't show yourself, for anything, understand? Got any snouts that can keep extra pairs of eyes out for you?'

'Yes sir. I think I know one or two who will help,' said Kettle.

'Shepherd and Perkins, I want you back here at six o'clock. I want you to work a late shift, in uniform again and show the Rookeries, nice and early, that you have not been put off,' said Charters.

'Yes, sir,' both replied.

'Sergeants Smith and Haynes, you know what you have to do?' said Charters.

'Yes sir. We'll grab a couple of hours shut eye and then we'll get back to our current task,' said Smith.

'I have had Sergeant Wright relieved at the Infirmary, and a constable will be with Mrs Black if she wakes and remembers anything else. Her son is down there with her and stinking the place out, vile man,' said Charters.

'Tonight, at nine o'clock, when the full night shift starts, I want you all back here. Then we will review our plans,' said Charters.

'Does that include us as well, sir?' said Shepherd.

'All of you, duties permitting. Knowing you two, there will probably be some other disaster befalling you between six and nine, if last night is anything to go by,' said Charters. 'Off you all go, quickly now!'

*****

About nine o'clock that morning, Shepherd walked through the door to his Aunt's house, on Twizzle and Twine Passage, where he and Sally now resided as man and wife. They had married in the great tradition of Christmas Morning, last, when residents of the Borough are married for free in the churches around the Borough. Constables could still not afford fancy trappings, and the job allowed Christmas morning church as free time, so it best suited all parties. Samson and Sally had married in St Mary de Castro, near Leicester Castle, on a crisp, white morning, with John Beddows acting as Samson's best man and John Flowers had given Sally away - her own parents long deceased. Samson's aunt was only too pleased to have young company, and when Samson was on duty, she and Sally kept good company together, apart from when Sally was out modelling for Mr Flowers' students.

'My goodness, Samson Shepherd; whatever has happened to you?' Sally cried out, as she saw the blood on Shepherd's clothing and cut across his cheek, before realizing part of his ear was now missing.

'We had a disagreement with a man with a rather sharp razor, and he caught me off-guard. Tom Hamilton has done the best he can, but I am going to look a bit odd from now onwards,' said Shepherd.

'This job gets more dangerous every day. Who was with you? Sergeant Beddows I suspect - getting you into more trouble?' said Sally.

'No, young Archie Perkins and I have been teamed up to resolve some problems around the Rookeries; just for a few days,' said Shepherd, trying to reassure her.

'Well he needs to be more careful and look after you!' said Sally, snapping harshly.

'Young Archie gave a very useful account of himself, I tell you. We were rather out-numbered and he stood his ground well. In fact, he looked like he was relishing things,' said Shepherd.

'He's still a boy, just a bit younger than you,' said Sally.

'Yes, but a ferocious little terrier with it,' said Shepherd. 'We will be fine.'

'You must be ready for some breakfast and a warm bed?' said Sally.

'A warm bed and then breakfast, I am exhausted, if you don't mind,' said Shepherd.

'I hate these duties,' said Sally. 'We never get time to speak anymore.'

Shepherd had already found a comfortable spot on his bed and was snoring before she had time to finish the statement.

'Who would be a constable's wife?' Sally asked Aunt Sarah.

'Better a constable's wife than a constable's widow, young Sally. Look after him and keep him safe; enjoy every minute you have together. I miss George so much at times like this!'

Chapter Seven – 'A blast from the past'

At about Midday, word started to spread that a well known and prominent face was being seen, travelling around amongst the Irish community within the Rookeries.

It was one of Herbert Kettle's snouts, who came to him with the news first.

'The Micks are saying that Sean Crowley has arrived back in town,' said the snout. 'Rumour has it, he is meeting with as many of the Irish leaders from around Green Street as he can muster, sometime later today.'

'Thanks for the nod,' said Kettle, deciding that a brisk walk back to the Station and a word with Mr Charters was a priority.

On his arrival, Mr Charters was at his desk, talking to Detective Sergeant Beddows.

'You look like you're in a hurry, Mr Kettle?' said Charters.

'You're not going to like this, sir. It appears that Sean Crowleys has turned up. Can't be a coincidence, with what's been going on?'

'What is the word on the streets?' said Beddows.

'Word is he is doing a tour of the Rookeries and arranging a meeting, later today. Sounds like a council of war!' replied Kettle.

'Might not be that bad. He will be an influence, no doubt about that. But we can use him in our favour, if we play our cards right,' said Charters.

'What are you thinking, sir?' said Beddows.

'We need to get down there and speak with him. Word alone around the Rookeries that he is back will put the fear of god into the incomers. We need to make sure that it stays at just that. I want you two down there and locate him. Talk to him and try and broker a solution,' said Charters.

'In that case, we'd better get down there right away,' said Beddows. 'This should be interesting, trying to get into the yards at this stage of events, from what Shepherd has been saying.'

*****

The two men looked out of place in the heart of the Rookeries. Beddows had still got his best grey woollen suit on, with his tie, tails and short topper. Kettle was still in his working scruffs, a flat cap, leather jerkin, and scruffy trousers and boots. The two looked like they should not be together, although one or two comments clearly suggested that people thought Kettle had been arrested and was being 'walked in'.

'Got your truncheon, John?' said Kettle, nervous at the thought of confrontations in the dark alleyways, even during the daylight, that they must venture into.

'Does it look like it?' said Beddows. 'You can't hide it very well in this suit. Last time I slid it down my trouser leg and the old lady leaped on me. I couldn't get out the house. Thought all her birthdays had come at once!'

'So is the answer yes or no?' said Kettle, anxiously.

'I have an alternative,' said Beddows. 'In fact, I was going to speak with Mr Charters and suggest it for all our detectives.'

'What's that then?' said Kettle.

'It looks a bit like my cock, but smaller, look...' said Beddows, reaching into the inner pocket of his coat, and producing a shorter hardwood truncheon, about twelve inches long, still with a leather strap through the handle. 'Got a mate of mine who makes furniture to knock me one up. It's much easier to carry when you're working in a suit.'

'Looks small!' said Kettle.

'You wait til you feel how heavy it is. Works a treat! One day we could all have something like it,' said Beddows.

'Can't see Mr Charters approving something that isn't issue,' said Kettle.

'Someone has to invent something for it to get used in the first place. It could make me a small fortune. Anyway, I'll worry about that if I have to use it,' said Beddows. 'Stop whining. By the way, where's yours then?'

'It's down the outside of my leg, as usual. Got the missus to put a new pocket down there to contain it,' said Kettle.

'Right then, let's find Mr Sean Crowley and find out what he's turned up for,' said Beddows.

*****

It didn't take the two men long to find more people milling around outside the alleyways along Abbey Street, Green Street and Orchard Street than in previous days. Confidence was obviously on the up already, just on the news alone.

A significant gathering outside the alleyway to Pork Shop Yard was a big clue that this was the likely whereabouts of Sean Crowley and his people. It was recognised that he was the natural successor to Dubh O'Donnell, but he had not yet assumed the position, much to the area's consternation. This might be the perfect time for him to assert his control.

As the two detectives approached the group, four bruisers detached themselves and walked towards them.

'And where the feck do you two think yers going?' said a very sharply dressed man, who appeared to have some influence over the others. 'Crushers, I can smell yers already! What business do yers have with Mr Crowley?'

'We're here to speak with Sean, privately. We have a proposition for him,' said Beddows.

'Sean is it? Mr Crowley's rather busy right now, so I'm sure he fecking well don't want to talk with yers right now,' said the bruiser.

'You go and tell Mr Crowley that Sergeant Beddows and a friend are here, and they have some business to discuss, urgently. I'm sure he will remember me,' said Beddows.

'Wait here then, while I go an' tell him,' said the bruiser. 'Be careful though, the natives are hungry, haven't eaten an Englishman for days.'

'They might bite off more than they can chew. Just go and tell your boss we're waiting,' said Beddows.

*****

After what seemed like ages, but in reality, had only been a few minutes, the man returned to the two detectives.

'Mr Crowley will see you now. Follow me,' said the bruiser, leading the way into Pork Shop yard and the perpetual darkness.

Three other bruisers fell in behind Beddows and Kettle, who kept touch of his truncheon, giving him a sense of added security, as the group squeezed down the narrow alley; passing the child prostitutes and drunks, and the dregs of Irish life who had little else to do, but exist in the putrid air and debris that this part of the Rookeries offered.

'Looking for a lady?' said a small and pitifully frail young girl, who could have been no more than ten, with limp, bright red hair, which with her weak brogue, signalled her heritage.

'It's pitiful,' said Kettle. 'What hope have these poor little bleeders got? She can't be more than ten at the most and selling her body already'.

'She's probably been at it for years,' said Beddows. 'We already know that kids are disposable down here – look at Dubh O'Donnell and his perverts'.

'Sick bastards,' said Kettle.

At the far end of the yard, which twisted and turned, creating a confusing run between the hovels, and at the opposite end to Abbey Street, stood the large, infamous, three story lodging house.

It would be a rare opportunity for Police to get inside the place without a pitched battle, which had been the norm in years gone by. It made Beddows nervous that they were being led in, without a fight. He felt like he was being led to slaughter, and a shiver ran down his spine, and thoughts of the Bower.

'Careful Kettle, this is not a comfortable feeling,' said Beddows.

'You watch my back and I'll watch yours,' said Kettle. 'Fingers crossed that he'll be okay.'

The ground floor of the lodging house was jammed full with an assortment of bruisers, ordinary folk, screaming babies, dogs, cats. The place smelled of ale and urine, and old rotting straw stuck to their feet, matted with bits of food and assorted excrement, as they walked along. At the front, stood on a chair, was Sean Crowley. Finely dressed, with a green, three piece suit and his trademark Derby hat, and with gold rings on each and every finger and tattoos visible around his neck, above his shirt collar, he looked a tough and well heeled adversary. Across the back wall was a sea of hard looking men, similarly well dressed. The bruisers of the area were back in strength, spurred on by Crowley's return. He was still a legend in the area, it seemed, and it would be a foolish bruiser to not respond to his call.

'Ah, Mr Beddows, seems like such a long time ago now? Remiss of me not to have renewed our acquaintance a little earlier, but I've been rather busy in the ole country,' said Crowley, voice straining above the noise of the crowd gathered in the room. 'And to what do I owe this pleasure?'

'We'd rather speak in private,' said Beddows.

'Here will be fine, from my perspective; never know what you rogues in the Police are up to,' said Crowley. 'These people will, I'm sure, be keen to hear what you have to offer me.'

'Word travels fast that you are back in the Borough, Mr Crowley, and we just wanted to make sure that everything was well in your world?' said Beddows. 'You left rather quickly the last time, and we didn't really get a chance to talk about your business intentions or interests.'

'Well now you have your chance, you and your colleague. What can I be doing for you?' said Crowley.

'Things have not been so good in the Irish community of late,' said Beddows.

'So I hear,' said Crowley. 'I'll have to make sure that it's put right.'

'That's what we want to talk about; putting things right. As much as it may seem strange, that is our wish also, to restore order and status quo,' said Beddows.

'Well it doesn't seem like you have been very interested so far, Mr Beddows. I hear tell that your boys have pretty much turned a blind eye just lately, and some of my friends here have had their arses kicked, a bit more than I like to hear,' said Crowley.

'That's probably been true of late, but as of the last couple of days, we've been turning things around a bit. My colleague, Constable Shepherd, who you will recall, is now going to look after the Rookeries and now him and me and others more like us, will not put up with the likes of the last few weeks,' said Beddows.

'It might just be a bit too late for that, now. I hear that there is a nest of rats sprung up since I left and they have been the cause of much of this unpleasantness. Rats should be put down, they are vermin; flea ridden vermin,' said Crowley, whose face now began to look more hostile.

'Word is going around the streets and alleyways surrounding the Rats' Castle that you are back, and they are already starting to talk. We know that they are very concerned, nervous even,' said Kettle.

'And so they should be; as I understand, a few of them are looking at following Dubh O'Donnell to get necked. Murdering old ladies, whatever next?' said Crowley, laughter breaking out in the gathered masses.

'They need to be taught a lesson, and that is our responsibility,' said Beddows. 'What we don't want is a war breaking out?'

'Do we look like an army, Mr Beddows? Basket makers, chip choppers and tinkers? Just simple folk, trying to live life in peace,' replied Crowley.

'I wasn't looking at them. I was looking at the numbers of Bruisers that suddenly seem to have reappeared with you - or for you,' said Beddows.

'It's nearly St Patrick's Day, Mr Beddows, and Leicester has one of the best ceili in England. We wouldn't have missed it for the world, now would we boys?'

'No!' came the resounding response, Irish voices raised and cheering wildly.

'The notion that you are back, has no doubt filled these incomers at the Rats' Castle with concern that you are here to displace them, yet again. With the work we're doing to take them down, bit by bit, brick by brick, we could make a useful alliance to restore peace in the Rookeries,' said Beddows.

'Whatever you say, Mr Beddows. You hear that, boys? There'll be no trouble, because the Police have told us so. What do you think, boys?' shouted Crowley.

Jeers filled the room, and shouts of 'death to the rats' rang out.

Kettle felt the hostility in the room increase and, momentarily, for the first time in his service, trapped in a most dangerous place. He visualized how he might escape through the maze of alleyways that separated him from the safety of Belgrave Gate and the wider streets and spaces.

'Now listen here,' shouted Sean Crowley. 'You people have to live here, and these gentlemen have to uphold the law. If we do what they ask, I'm sure things will be a little easier for yers all in the future, Isn't that right, Mr Beddows? So, let's have no stupidity. Me and the boys will make sure nobody comes looking for trouble in our alleyways and yards, and our pubs and shops, and then we can all enjoy the 17th in peace.'

'So you will not look to take the law into your own hands?' said Beddows.

'We'll keep the peace down here, if you promise to get rid of the rats! You scratch our backs and we'll scratch yours, get rid of the rats and their fleas once and for all though,' said Crowley.

'We can't ask for any more than that,' said Kettle.

'Not at the moment, anyway,' said Beddows, not wishing to offer Crowley free reign over the area.

'We'll put the word round that we think something's brewing. That will keep them nervous, whilst we decide how to take out the ringleaders. Just keep to your end of the bargain Mr Crowley, and keep out of their territory, for the time being,' said Beddows.

'Mr Beddows, all I want is for my little businesses to get back to order, for my pubs and warehouses to be full again, and for these poor people to have a happy and quiet life once again. If working together keeps that arrangement in place, then you have my word that we'll do as you ask.'

'In that case, we'll let you get back to your business,' said Beddows.

******

'Do you believe a word of what Crowley promised?' said Charters.

'To be honest, sir, I have no confidence in him at all. He is a feared man in the Irish Community, as he is in the rest of the Rookeries. He has come back with all the muscle he could muster, by the look of it. And some of Dubh O'Donnell's boys have appeared out of the woodwork to show their new found allegiance to him,' said Beddows.

'We haven't heard from Sergeants Smith or Haynes yet, as they are otherwise engaged. What news from around Sandacre Street, Mr Kettle?'

'My snouts say that the place is still full to overflowing, and nobody has left. Nobody turned up for the hearing of the five prisoners this morning, which was a bit of a surprise. Probably still don't want to come out of their lair.'

'So, the rats are still in their nest? I don't want to go in, if we can draw them out,' said Charters.

'I have a feeling that they might be licking their wounds. Five of their sort in Gaol, and thinking they've botched the job at Cock Muck Hill,' said Beddows.

'I don't want a war, or even a battle. We can't be seen to let that happen. We know the men we want, and we would prefer to detain them outside of their stronghold,' said Charters. 'Once they are locked up and we can clear out the Rats' Castle, the Irish will have nobody to fight but themselves again, or us.'

'I have an idea,' said Beddows. 'Are you feeling reckless again, Herbert, my old mate?'

'What do you have in mind this time, Beddows?' said Charters.

'What about inviting the chief rats to a meeting with their various counterparts, a parlez?' said Beddows.

'How are you going to get them out?' said Charters.

'What if somebody else invites them? What if the Cock Muck Hill boys invite them both, the rats and the Irish, to discuss a truce?' said Beddows.

'Can't see them falling for that,' said Kettle. 'Not if they think they killed the old lady. Porky's lot wouldn't hear of it.'

'They're such an arrogant lot, they might want to turn up just to size up the opposition,' said Beddows. 'Well, what if Kettle and I turn up and announce ourselves as part of the Cock Muck Hill boys? We can see what the reaction is and take it from there,' said Beddows.

'Let's have everyone sleep on it tonight, see what happens, then we'll have a look at it again in the morning, first thing,' said Charters.

'What do we do tonight?' said Beddows.

'Shepherd and Perkins are back at six. We brief them on events surrounding both the rats and Sean Crowley, and we see what rumour and gossip comes out overnight. Smith and Haynes will be busy tonight, I suspect, and will have their eyes and ears open in the right places.'

Chapter Eight – 'Long live the King'

At six o'clock on Tuesday 4th March, Shepherd and Perkins sat with Beddows, Kettle, Smith and Haynes in the back office at the Town Hall Station. The men were updated as to the events surrounding Aggie Black, the rats and Sean Crowley.

'So, it could be an interesting night down in the Rookeries, tonight?' said Shepherd.

'Could be bastard hell, pardon my French,' said Perkins, grinning widely.

'Is there something wrong with you?' said Beddows. 'I've never seen anyone seem so excited at the prospect of fighting and the threat of getting your head kicked in.'

'If you'd been brought up like me, it gets taken for granted. I was an orphan, Mr Beddows and have not had a happy life. Some of the folk that took me in were nice, but most couldn't afford me and many treated me like a punch-bag. I ain't afraid of anyone anymore, as I've always had to stand up for myself.'

'Didn't mean to pry Perkins, but you worry me at times, with your bravado,' said Beddows.

'Don't you worry about me, any of you. Life is for living and I'm going to be here for a long time yet, but nobody is going to put me down again, ever! Not Archie Perkins.'

'You mind you don't go getting someone else killed with your recklessness,' said Tanky Smith. 'Hard little bugger you might think you are at the moment, but there's always someone bigger and harder and unpredictable. Just slow down a bit. I'm telling you from experience.'

'You don't get a face like Tanky's without experience!' laughed Black Tommy.

'I'll keep him on a tight leash,' said Shepherd. 'Sally would never forgive me if I got killed'.

'Too bleeding late then,' said Beddows.

'So what should we be on the lookout for tonight? Mr Charters obviously wants us treading on toes still?' said Shepherd.

'Tommy and me will be about tonight, but you won't notice us, and nor should they,' said Tanky Smith. 'We aren't expecting our blokes back from Birmingham 'til tomorrow, so we have some other ideas tonight. I reckon you'd do best keeping an eye on the Irish yards, see whether there are any signs of confidence returning, or of a show of strength, straying out of their shitholes now Crowley's back.'

'What about the Rats' Castle?' said Perkins.

'Leave that well alone. We have plans for tomorrow for them! Keep out of Bateman's Row and Sandacre Street, unless you really have to,' said Black Tommy.

'What about you two, Mr Beddows? You and Mr Kettle?' said Perkins.

'We've got a bit of a pub crawl in mind for tonight. A cup of tea or lemonade for me in every pub along both sides of Belgrave Gate, I think. Mr Kettle will be on halves, and I will be seen pushing him back in a wheelbarrow, somewhere about eleven, if he sticks to halves like he says!' said Beddows.

'Belgrave Gate - in a wheelbarrow? More like a hearse if the bruisers see fit,' laughed Haynes. 'Don't go upsetting them now they're back in town.'

'I suspect they will be in fine fettle, celebrating Sean Crowley's return and will be in no mood for going on the offensive tonight,' said Beddows.

'Got your new toy, Beddows?' enquired Tanky.

'New toy?' said Beddows.

'A little bird tells me you've had your cock modelled into an offensive weapon? If that's right, there won't be much left to hit people with when you've got your big mitts wrapped about it,' said Tanky, winking.

'I'll have you know, that I have shown it to Mr Charters and he is actually, very impressed' said Beddows.

'Probably so, but when are you going to show him your new truncheon?' said Black Tommy, giggling like a little girl.

'Ho, Ho, Ho!' said Beddows, taking Shepherd's lead of walking into sucker punches.

'Mind you,' said Tanky, 'If you waved your cock about at me it would probably frighten me off rather quick, from what I've heard; probably more so than your new toy.'

'Come on Perkins, you and I have streets to patrol,' said Shepherd. 'Our detectives have far too much time on their hands'.

*****

By six thirty, the dusk was setting in. March was still a damp month, and the ever increasing soot and smoke in the Borough's air seemed to bring darkness earlier than anywhere else for miles around.

The factories and foundries were still in full production, and shops were closed, so those milling around on the streets were either very well off, on their way to an evening of fun and frivolity, or were very poor, and looking for any slightest opportunity to beg, steal or take advantage of the rich ones.

Carts and carriages of every shape and size still filled the streets, with delivery men coming and going, and the odd coach moving on and off the stage post at the Stag and Pheasant in Humberstone Gate.

Lamps were lit in the pubs and gin palaces all over the Borough, and the landlords and landladies would be busy watering down their stocks in anticipation of fleecing the drunker clientele, later on.

Wednesdays were cattle and sheep fair day in the town and a few herdsmen and farmers from the edge of the County were starting to arrive early. Cattle and sheep could be heard in the area of the Cattle Market on Horse Fair Street. The beasts would be penned overnight, and the herdsmen would be found in the local pubs such as 'The Saracen's Head', or down in or off Humberstone Gate at 'The Admiral Nelson', or 'The Champion', striking early deals with slaughter-men and butchers who would gather there, perhaps even 'The Artillery Man' if an odd pig or two had been brought in with them.

Tomorrow would be a busy day, and Shepherd prayed that tonight would be a lot calmer.

*****

By eight o'clock, the area around Abbey Street and Green Street was clearly back to its old self. Far more of the 'common' Irish population had ventured out of their hovels in the surrounding streets and yards and alleyways.

It was times like this when Shepherd could see why the area had been given the name 'Rookeries' as on every low wall, pavement, shop step, and parked cart, were sitting groups of men, women and children.

The air was thick with tobacco smoke, and everyone, from young children, upward, seemed to have their Dudeens alight, as they hunkered together, talking and yelling. Irish songs broke the monotony of their brogue every once in a while, and strains of 'The Wild Rover' which was always good for joining in, or 'Johnny I hardly knew Ye', an anti-war song that the Irish that had served in the British East India Company brought back with them.

Mixed in amongst them were pairs of bruisers, making their presence clear, with their sharp suits and bowler hats, and large gold rings adorning gnarled fighters' hands.

There was a message in the crowds tonight. *The Irish are back!*

'Don't think anyone will want to be messing with this lot tonight?' said Perkins.

'I think you might be right, Perkins. And we need to make our presence known, but not antagonize them, understand? Whatever they may say to provoke, ignore it.'

At the entrance to Pork Shop Yard stood Sean Crowley, surrounded by his personal bruisers, the biggest and hardest of the lot. Crowley was attracting the attention attributed to Royalty, and everyone seemed to want to say hello. He was playing the game and winning the support he knew he would need to be the top dog in the Rookeries.

Later, no doubt, he would be sizing up his business empire and muscling in at 'The King George III' and 'The Horse Breakers', before renewing his acquaintance with the hag, Clodagh Murphy, down at 'The Fox and Grapes', persuading her that Dubh was dead and he would now be the man to pay 'protection'.

'How long would they have to wait, before 'The Stokers Arms' would open again with its lights burning bright?' Shepherd pondered.

'Good evening, Constable Shepherd,' said Crowley.

'You remember me then, Mr Crowley?' said Shepherd.

'I always remember potential adversaries or threats; makes for good business sense,' said Crowley.

'Adversaries or threats? How might you think that of me?' said Shepherd.

'I saw the way you behaved during your problems with Mr O'Donnell; word around the Fancy was that you were a little more of a threat than most of your colleagues. If you weren't a constable, I could offer you a good life as one of my boys,' said Crowley.

'That's a very kind thought, Mr Crowley, but I am happy with my lot at the present,' said Shepherd.

'How's the old ear tonight?' said Crowley, admiring the neat stitching.

'It still hears what it needs, Mr Crowley, and it remains open, constantly,' said Shepherd. 'Are you planning on staying a little longer again this time?'

'I'm off to see my Ma and Pa at the Borough Gaol tomorrow, and see what they say. I have a few old friends to look up, and some business interests to resolve, and then I'll see. Who's your friend, by the way? Rude of me not to say hello.'

'Constable Perkins, Mr Crowley, and not offended, I'm sure,' said Perkins.

'Ah, the other pugilist I've been hearing about. Some of Dick Cains' boys rate you quite highly Mr Perkins. Hear you've put Mr Shepherd here on his arse a couple of times. Can't be bad,' said Crowley, smirking.

'You don't want to offer me a job then?' asked Perkins, cockily.

'Cheeky young upstart. You never know - one day?' said Crowley.

'Shame, I'm just like Shepherd here, once a constable, always a constable.'

'More than can be said of some of your colleagues. Sounds like one or two have been trying to drink me dry of late,' said Crowley.

'Bad apples in every barrel,' said Shepherd, 'as I am sure you will find in your own barrels.'

'Not for long in my case though,' said Crowley. 'They tend to attract rats, and that won't do!'

'Rats not good for business then, Mr Crowley?' said Shepherd.

'Not at present, it would seem; but I understand the Borough Rat catchers are busy laying a trap?' said Crowley.

'Is that right?' said Perkins. 'Where did you hear that then?'

'Mr Beddows and Mr Kettle suggested I leave the rats alone whilst they sort things out,' said Crowley.

'Sounds like a good plan to me,' said Shepherd.

'Will be alright if the rats are still around when you try and eliminate them,' said Crowley.

'I don't suspect they'll be looking to trouble you again, not after this display tonight?' said Shepherd.

'Yes, quite impressive, nice to see Irish folks at ease on our own streets again.'

'If they're happy, and you're happy, we're happy,' said Perkins.

'And long may it remain so, Mr Perkins. And now I must be off, places to go and all that.'

'Goodnight to you then, Mr Crowley, and no doubt we'll be seeing a bit more of each other for a while at least?' said Shepherd.

'And so we will,' said Crowley, 'so we will!'

*****

In Cock Muck Hill, the Parish Guardians had sent carpenters to repair the six almshouses after last night's attack. Two men were still working, one fitting small squares of thick glass, and one tapping lead strips back into the frames.

Stood in the yard between the hovels was a small group of men, who looked up at the approach of the two constables.

'Any news of Porky?' said one. 'He's not been back all day?'

'I think he's taken it badly, to be honest,' said Shepherd. 'How are the old folk?'

'My dad's gutted. He's realised his medals have gone. I need to tell Sergeant Beddows,' said the man.

'What's your dad's name?' said Perkins.

'Henry Williams. His medals are from his time in Afghanistan, and they mean the world to him. One belongs to his brother who never came back.'

'We'll let Mr Beddows know,' said Perkins.

'What about the others?' said Shepherd.

'They're a bit happier. They've had their doors and windows fixed, and a few of us have brought some old furniture where theirs got broke. Mayor Harris sent some extra coal round as a gesture from the Borough, not much, but earlier than expected,' said the man.

'No signs of trouble tonight?' said Shepherd.

'Not now the Irish are back out, we should all be left alone, I would hope,' said the man.

'Fingers crossed,' said Perkins.

*****

At ten o'clock, Beddows and Kettle were in their sixth pub of the evening, checking out with snouts, or simply listening to what conversation they were party to before people realised they were Police. There were few in the category of 'didn't recognise them' as most of the pubs were full of regular patrons, predominantly Irish bruisers, 'Fancy' or hangers on. The 'working class' Irish were still hard at work, and would start to filter in as Corahs and Star Foundry and other such large, new, enterprises closed their doors any moment soon.

The same conversations were taking place in all the pubs - and all the talk was of Sean Crowley. Everyone had seemed to have now overlooked and forgiven his absence for the last twelve months.

Herbert Kettle had now joined Beddows on Lemonade, or rather 'Schweppes' effervescent Lemonade' which was by now highly regarded, globally it was said, as a health tonic, or else their ginger beer.

Several licensees teased the men as being soft, not proper, hard drinking constables, like the others they had in through their back doors. However, they were tolerated.

Rumour seemed to be that tomorrow, Crowley was off to visit his Ma and Pa at the Borough Gaol, and then afterwards he had convened a 'business meeting' at the old 'Stokers Arms', sometime after two o'clock.

Everything suggested the Irish were enjoying a night of freedom and celebration, for the first time in nearly a year. Having Crowley and his bruisers around, gave them a huge sense of relief.

By eleven Beddows and Kettle were back at the Station and briefing Mr Charters, with no need for any wheelbarrows along the way.

At seven o'clock the next morning, Shepherd and Perkins walked back into the Station, complaining that it had been a long, cold and boring night duty, and that calm seemed to have returned to the Rookeries.

Chapter Nine – 'No such thing as a free breakfast'

At seven thirty a.m. on Wednesday 5th March, there appeared peace and tranquility in the Rookeries.

The Irish had made merry all night, protected by Sean Crowley's boys.

The Cock Muck Hill defence company had all slept sound, knowing their relatives were again secure, and a little warmer and more comfortable.

In the Rats' Castle, Cox and his cronies, were lying around in various states of hangover, still deciding whether to brass it out, or do a runner. Their spies had advised them that the Irish were no longer docile and had a very heavy presence, which Cox would have to think twice about mixing it with.

The yards and alleyways were void of women and kids, who slept in huddles in their small, squalid rooms. Only dogs and cats, and the odd wily rat, scurried around in the rubbish and left-overs that were being chewed or carried off.

Back at Town Hall Station, Mr Charters was up and about, and had been joined by Tanky Smith and Black Tommy Haynes. Beddows and Kettle joined them within minutes. Shepherd and Perkins updated the men on the overnight news, and this was corroborated by Smith and Haynes, who had been incognito in some yard or other and with one of the lesser gangs around Sandacre Street or Gravel Lane.

'Tommy and me can't stop long, Mr Charters. We have a little business to finish off, first thing,' said Tanky Smith. 'I know just what you mean,' said Charters. 'You get off and sort that out. Let us know later what is happening.'

The early shift had paraded and marched out and were now making their patrols, shaking door handles and windows, scrounging breakfast, in some form or other, and probably a few babies would be made before their first point of the day. The Rookeries were quiet and would not be bothered by uniforms until later in the day, other than showing the flag around the periphery. Sergeant Wright was, for a change, duty Station 'Charge' Sergeant. His cells were empty, unusually.

'Don't like this, sir,' said Wright. 'I've never known the town so quiet of a night duty; not even a bunter or drunk for Mr Hildyard from the *charged* cell.'

'Seems like the calm before the storm,' said Beddows. 'That's what worries me more.'

*****

A short while later, a large, canvas covered butcher's wagon pulled into Sandacre Street. Its driver slowed down, moving along towards Bateman's Row, straining to see names of premises. It bore the name 'Brady's of Loughborough - Butchers' in fading pale coloured lettering on the side, and smelled of strong rancid meat, as such wagons do after years of bloody carcasses and the like, which leak into the joints and knots.

The wagon was high sided, and enclosed by its dark canvas top, painted a horrible maroon colour and looked like it had seen better days, much like the old nag that pulled it.

The driver looked lost and confused as it pulled to a halt at the front of the entrance to Bateman's Yard.

One of Cox's henchmen, standing guard at the entrance, called across at the driver, 'What are you looking for squire, you look lost?'

'I'm not from around these parts, I'm looking for Green Street, I've got two whole cattle carcasses for a Mr

Crowley, for a party tonight,' said the driver, in a soft Irish brogue.

'Hang on a minute squire; I'll get someone who can show you where it is.' The man ran off and into the darkness of the yard. Another man took his place; only one.

'Cox, wake up; you'll never believe this. There's some idiot butcher outside, with a wagon full of beef for some bloke in Green Street, for a party tonight,' said the original lookout.

Cox's eyes lit up, and he quickly stood and stretched. 'That'll be beef for the Irish feller that's come to town. Wouldn't it be a shame if it didn't turn up as expected?' said Cox.

'What you thinking?' said Phillips, the Welshman, stirring.

'Come on lads, on your feet, we'll all eat like kings for a week!'

Grabbing up various knives and hammers that were lying around, seven or eight of the rats that still remained, led by Cox himself, made haste to the wagon.

'Get down from the bleeding wagon, mate,' said Cox, shouting at the driver. 'Lose yerself if you know what's good for you. We'll take care of your beef now!'

The man climbed down and stood on the side next to Cox. 'It's for Green Street, and if it don't get there, they'll flay me alive, so I hear.'

'Well tell your boss you got robbed,' said Cox, making a straight line for the rear of the wagon.

As he started to open it, the flaps burst outwards, and big, hard looking men started jumping down, all shouting and waving cudgels, large sticks with bulbous heads.

The first man out grabbed Cox by the throat and pushed him hard into the alleyway towards the Rats' Castle. The man in the alleyway started shouting as he turned to run in and warn the other occupants, but he was hit brutally from behind and fell down.

Cox was now on the floor inside the alley, and as he looked up, he saw the bulbous head of the man's club coming straight at his face, and it smashed in hard, once, twice. Pain came, and then darkness.

'And there's you - thinking you were in for a free breakfast. Fecking rats. This is one for the Irish!'

There were now ten men, including the driver, and all of them stormed up the alleyway, and into the Rats' Castle, which was now insecure and unguarded, apart from the men who had gone with Cox, who were all now being given a beating of their lives.

Phillips tried to defend himself, pulling out a curved fighting knife, which he had picked up somewhere or other on his war travels, flailing it wildly at his attackers. But it was a futile gesture, as he too, fell victim to the bulbous clubs, his head split open and then his kneecaps smashed.

The sounds of heads and arms breaking, and men screaming as other knees were deliberately smashed, filled the occupants inside the Rats' Castle with terror. Women and children screamed, as they sought exit from the assault on their men.

Fighting dogs started to snap and bite at the attackers, stoutly defending their masters, but they too were beaten, in most cases to death!

Within four or five minutes, the battle for the Rats' Castle was over. Not one of the male occupants who were old enough or offered age and metal to resist the attack, were standing. Cox, Phillips and several others, many unconscious, and with horrific head injuries, broken arms and smashed kneecaps, were unceremoniously dragged out onto the front of

Bateman's Row, where they were tied to the wheels of the butchers wagon.

One or two large men checked the bindings, before giving each of the 'prisoners' further violent kicks in the head and body. There appeared no concern that these men could be killed in doing so.

'That'll teach yers to feck with Mr Crowley's people!' said the leader of the men from the van, spitting a huge wad of phlegm over the face of the badly injured Cox.

'You girl,' shouted the man, to a young girl of about nine or ten; 'Now be a good girl, and go and find a constable and tell them someone has hurt your daddy.'

The attackers then walked confidently away and into the heart of the Rookeries, and no doubt the safety of the Irish Community.

*****

News spread quickly, as the first constable on the scene swung his rattle in earnest, and word spread that something brutal had taken place at the Rats' Castle.

Chapter Ten – 'Rats on the run'

Charters, Beddows and Kettle made their way from Town Hall Lane together, as the news broke.

By now, most of the constables and sergeants of the early shift were there or were in reserve nearby.

On their arrival, the men were still tied to the wagon. One or two were regaining consciousness and the whole area was filled with screaming and crying women and children and barking dogs.

Charters ordered the uniformed constables to take the women and children back into Bateman's Yard and out of the way, until they could be spoken to.

A local surgeon, William Cunningham, from the dispensary on Charles Street, had been making his way to work from Pasture Lane. He had stopped, and was trying to administer treatment to stop bleeding, splint fractures or revive the unconscious. Lacking dispensary supplies, which would normally be supplied at a cost, he had sent the women into their hovels to fetch anything that could be torn into bandages, or lengths of wood that could be used as splints. He had served as a young medic at Trafalgar, and some of the injuries were as brutal as any he had seen in hand to hand combat.

He had left the men tethered as he was unsure of the significance. That, he would leave to the Police to work out.

Two scruffy, shady looking individuals approached the scene. They were seen by one of the conscious Rats' Castle gang, who called out, 'Brooksy, Isaac, leg it, quick or they'll hang you, too.'

Before they could run, they were grabbed, forcefully by Beddows and Kettle.

'Oh no you don't,' said Beddows. 'You'll be coming with us, I rather think!'

'Gentlemen, before you are taken away, I want to know who these men are?' said Charters, indicating the men tied to the wheels of the wagon.

'That one is Cox; He is Phillips; the one that's awake is Davies; they are the ones from Cock Muck Hill, and Phillips is the one who did old Porky's mother,' said Brooks.

'Were they all involved in the Cock Muck Hill job?' said Charters

'All of the ones who did the job are there. The others are thieves and conmen, and we have been getting rid of their proceeds,' said Isaac the Jew.

'I take it these are Sergeant Smith's inside men?' said Kettle.

'Yes,' said Charters. 'I want them out of the way, as soon as possible.'

'You bastards, grassing us all up - you'll hang as well you know!' shouted Davies.

'Right, I want all these man arrested, and taken in to the cells. We'll have a surgeon look at them later,' said Charters.

Health care was a matter for individuals, and if you couldn't pay for it, you didn't get it - Broken heads, arms, legs and all!

'Sergeant Kettle, get two constables to take statements from all the women and children that can tell us anything. We have to investigate the attack, but I also realise that these same men are also our suspects, and have been delivered to us in one fell go. I suspect there may be some punishment element to play here and I wouldn't look too far to see who is behind it!' said Charters.

'What about me, sir?' said Beddows.

'You can concentrate on these prisoners to start off with. I will get Smith and Haynes in shortly. Kettle, once you have sorted out the constables, come back to the station,' said Charters.

'How are we getting them back?' said Beddows.

'We've been left a horse and wagon, and that is our transport. We can put it in the yard at 'The King and Crown' whilst we find out where it has come from. Take enough constables to secure them.'

'What about you, sir?' said Beddows.

'I'm going to bother Mr Goodyer, as some enquiries need to be made in the County by the look of things and they can perhaps help us with extra manpower for a couple of hours.'

*****

By ten o'clock Kettle and Beddows were summoned to Mr Charter's office.

Shortly after, there was a knock on the door, and Sergeant Wright brought in the two men, Brooks and Isaac the Jew, who had been sat in one of the cells with the least injured prisoners, separated from the others in the two larger cells.

'Ah, gentlemen, I was becoming a little worried that you had arrived at the Rats' Castle earlier than expected and would be among our list of casualties,' said Charters.

'Wouldn't have got back from Small Heath that quick; planned on getting back to Rats' Castle about nine,' said Brooks, looking across and winking at the old, scruffy Jew, stood alongside him.

Isaac the Jew looked at Kettle, and slowly pulled the large hooked nose off his face, and lifted the wig, beard and black brimmed hat. 'Amazing what you can do with a bit of paste, a mask and a wig.'

'Hells bells, it's you, Haynes,' said Kettle.

'So it is,' said Black Tommy, running his fingers through his own jet black, wavy hair.

'Morning, Kettle,' said Brooks, the man with the grey beard, which also came away, revealing Tanky Smith.

'Morning chaps,' said Beddows. 'You and your dressing up box; you get better with every job you work!'

'I thought Isaac the Jew was a real fence, he's been around for months?' said Kettle.

'So he has,' said Haynes, 'but alas, it appears his cover is now blown!'

'Well I'll be!' said Kettle, shaking his head. 'Never would have recognised you.'

'That's how we prefer it,' said Tanky Smith. 'Less chance of being made out!'

'So what are the prisoners saying?' said Charters.

'They're all in terrible pain. It was definitely the Irish, and it's a punishment. Nice for us though, cos it's saved us having to draw them out of the Castle,' said Tanky Smith. 'They all think they're for the Gallows, and want Phillips to confess on his own, or they'll grass him up.'

'Sergeant Beddows, what about the worse injuries?' said Charters.

'Cox and another chap are just waking up. Dr Buck is here and says they might be lucky to have such thick skulls, but nearly every one of them has had his kneecaps smashed. He wants them at the Infirmary, if they can pay.'

'Life's is so unfair' said Charters, cynically. 'They're prisoners now, and will soon be in the care of the Governor of the Borough Gaol. It will be their own making, and they will have to make do like every other poor soul has to who can't afford to pay - suffer!'

'One day, someone will say we have to treat them fair,' said Haynes.

'If that day ever comes, then that's when we'll start,' said Charters. 'In the meantime, they're criminals and scum, and that's how we'll treat them.'

'When are we going to tell them that old Mrs Black is alive?' said Beddows.

'You can break the good news when you charge them. Let them sweat, as well as hurt!' said Charters, who was not a great supporter of leniency.

'What are the women saying, Mr Kettle?' said Charters.

'They all say that it was the Irish. Supposedly there were about ten of them, and they jumped out of the back of the wagon. The driver had pulled up, saying he was lost, and that he had two carcasses of beef for a Mr Crowley in Green Street. Cox decided to 'divert' the beef, but when he and his men got to the back of the wagon, the Irish jumped out and beat hell out of them all. They all had big knobbly clubs,' said Kettle.

'Ah, the wooden horse of Troy,' said Charters.

'The wooden horse of where?' said Kettle.

'Have you never read any classics, you heathen?' said Charters.

'I don't read at all, never have time or the inclination, too busy working!' said Kettle.

'Heathen!' said Smith and Haynes, simultaneously.

'At least I can read,' said Kettle.

'And we just get dressed up and play detectives?' said Tanky Smith.

'Bloody good job you do, too,' said Beddows. 'And by the way, those big knobbly clubs are called Shillelaghs, and that does suggest they were Irish.'

'Another expert?' said Haynes.

'Had one round my bonce once, at 'The Fox and Grapes' and by old Clodagh herself, years back when we went to bring in her husband.'

'I can see now, why Shepherd gets clobbered so often. Learned everything from you, did he?' said Tanky Smith, laughing loudly.

*****

For most of the day, the Station was full with the cries and screams from the injured prisoners. Apart from some leather strap-like 'bites' that Mr Buck had managed to hand out, there was nothing that would take away the pain. So, like everyone else, they were left to suffer. Broken bones were splinted and bandaged, but many of these men would unlikely walk on their own, ever again.
Most Physicians still believed that pain was a symptom and generally indicated that a patient must be alive and apparently well. A lack of pain was more dangerous. Suffering was therefore something to be welcomed.
Beddows admired those Physicians!

*****

At six o'clock Shepherd and Perkins returned to duty. Shepherd had already heard that something had happened. Sally had been shopping and the town was alive with stories of a fierce battle and horrendous injuries, like those at Trafalgar.
It would not take a lot of guessing the source of the stories, which quickly spread in the queues amongst those sat outside the People's Dispensary on Charles Street.
Mr Charters assembled his men, once again. Beddows, Kettle, Smith, Haynes, Shepherd and Perkins and took them across to his house at the rear of the yard.

'We have to tread very carefully now,' said Charters. 'Today, there was a punishment beating in Bateman's Row, no doubt, conducted by a group of Irish. Mr Goodyer confirms that the butcher's wagon was stolen from Loughborough sometime yesterday, from an Irish butcher named Mahoney. He doesn't want to complain. In the course of the beating, we have had the persons responsible for the attacks in Cock Muck Hill handed to us on a platter. I suspect that it was an intended outcome.'

'Do you think Sean Crowley is behind it?' said Shepherd.

'We have no doubt, between us, that Sean Crowley would have instigated it,' said Charters.

'However,' said Beddows 'We are not going to have any witnesses to complain. The Rats' Castle boys we have locked up are not saying anything, other than it was some Irish boys. They also know they are all going to Gaol. Most think they are going to get their necks stretched, as we have not yet felt the need to tell them Mrs Black is alive, nor charged them yet.'

'What about the women and sprogs back at The Rats' Castle?' said Shepherd.

'They are packing up their sad, meagre belongings and saying they are going back to London, as soon as they can get out. There are wagons outside already loading up their junk. None of them will say a word, as they're now terrified, without their men,' said Kettle.

'So, Sean Crowley's going to get away with it?' said Perkins.

'If there's no complaint, and nobody will say who they were, or identify anyone, there's nothing to get away with,' said Beddows.

'Anyone told Porky Black yet?' said Kettle.

'I was leaving that for you,' said Charters. 'I understand he is very fond of you, Mr Kettle?'

'We have an understanding,' said Kettle.

'What do you want Perkins and me to do, sir?' said Shepherd.

'You'd better get down there and patrol the Rookeries. See what is being said and done on the streets,' said Charters. 'I rather hope and suspect you might be in for a quiet night.'

Chapter Eleven – 'A return to normality?'

Six thirty saw Shepherd and Perkins, yet again, walk the route down to the Rookeries, passing by colleagues on their normal routine, much to their annoyance. The resentment that was created when Mr Charters selected Shepherd and Perkins for this job was that intense it could now almost be reached out and touched.

There was still, sadly, an apathy and malaise in 1851, within the Borough Force. After Detective Sergeant Roberts' demise that April previous, a few rotten apples had bobbed to the top, but there were as many still there, scroungers and skivers, who would never want to take a risk and make Policing an honourable job.

Shepherd and Perkins were seen as Robert Charters' 'favourites' and would never be trusted by many. They were a danger, and would turn in those who failed to do the job.

'Feels like we've trod in something disgusting,' said Perkins.

'You've noticed it too?' said Shepherd.

'They don't like it when you actually do the job properly do they?' said Perkins.

'You'll get used to it,' said Shepherd. 'You just need to grow a thick skin'.

'So, where are we off to tonight?'

'Sandacre Street to start off with; I want to see how this lot are getting on with their packing, and I want to know when they've actually gone. Our lives will be a lot less stressful,' said Shepherd.

'Then where?'

'We'll visit the Mansfield Head. We need to make it clear that rules are rules and that by eleven at night, the lights will go off, and the doors will be locked,' said Shepherd.

'And then?'

'Why are you so keen to know where we are going?' said Shepherd.

'You have a most organised mind, Shepherd. Nothing is spontaneous. Ever thought of doing something spontaneous?'

'I thought about it once, but I had something else to do first,' laughed Shepherd.

'Ha-Ha; Very funny!'

'Remember, this is still the Rookeries, and it's still a place we're less than welcome on most streets, even today!' said Shepherd. 'So, keep vigilant. There will be some very angry rats along the roads, and there may be some nervous Irish, waiting to see how we respond to their actions.'

'Okay,' said Perkins.

'We'll have a wander around Abbey Street and Green Street, and no doubt Sean Crowley will pop up and test us. Then I want to pop into Cock Muck Hill and let the old folk know we are about'.

'That's a lot to do?'

'That's what we're here for, and for the whole of the night duty,' said Shepherd.

*****

There seemed a frantic scurry in Sandacre Street, and along Bateman's Row, as groups of women and children were loading piles of poor quality furniture and personal belongings onto rickety carts, which would be drawn by equally rickety mules or horses. If their intention was to return to London and their old stamping grounds, Shepherd hoped they had some stopping off points along the way.

Younger men or more accurately, boys in their early teens, were doing much of the labouring and physical work, whilst the older women organised and pointed, shouting and swearing continuously.

'You bastards could have protected us, now look at what you've done,' screamed a woman who Shepherd recognised from outside the Mansfield Head the night before last, urging the men to fight.

'And you've changed your tune,' shouted Perkins.

'Don't be drawn by them, Perkins, that's what they want you to do,' said Shepherd.

'Leaving your men behind and scurrying off, just like the rats you live like?' shouted a passing local. 'Good riddance to the lot of you. Naught but trouble since you got here.'

'And you can clear off, too,' shouted Perkins. 'Mind your own business.'

Shepherd saw one or two large well dressed men standing at the end of Gravel Lane, making sure the rats were actually leaving. Nothing was said. Their presence alone said enough to unsettle the remaining rats.

'You seen them two down at the end, near Gravel Lane?' said Perkins.

'Saw them a moment or two ago. Reinforcers, I would suggest. Just need to be seen to get the message across, once and for all. I bet this lot are shitting themselves. What else can happen to them, they'll be thinking?' said Shepherd.

'Surprised they didn't burn them out, and finish the job off,' said Perkins.

'They didn't need to, not after punishment like they dished out,' said Shepherd.

'I suppose once they've gone, there'll be a new lot come along?' said Perkins.

'There aren't enough lodging houses in the Borough as it is. The Borough will let it to some new landlord, and they'll fill it with whoever stumbles into Leicester next,' said Shepherd.

'I bet the Micks will have a say in it,' said Perkins.

'Mr Crowley has probably already got a landlord lined up!' said Shepherd. 'Anyway, let's move on to the Mansfield Head. Have a word with the licensee.'

*****

At about seven thirty, the Mansfield Head was closed. No lights were on, and the place was quiet.

'Strange,' said Shepherd.

'Shall we go round the back?' said Perkins.

'Go on then.'

In the yard at the back was the licensee, Edward Martin. His nose looked like it had recently been broken, and his two eyes were dark and swollen. A split bottom lip dripped blood onto his white shirt.

'Looks like you've met with some bad luck?' said Shepherd.

'Fell over the dog,' said Martin, kicking out at a scabby mongrel, that scurried about at his feet.

'So, not opening tonight?' said Perkins.

'Not tonight. Anyway, looks like most of my customers are either locked up or packing up and buggering off,' said Martin.

'Sure you don't want to make a complaint?' said Shepherd.

'For what?' said Martin.

'Won't force you, if you don't want to,' said Shepherd.

'Do you really think I'm that stupid? Don't think there's much prospect of staying down here and doing much trade. Thinking about a place in the countryside somewhere,' said Martin.

'Probably for the best?' said Perkins, trying to be sympathetic.

'If you lot had done your job properly in the first place, we'd all have been alright. You let the incomers take over, and now we're all paying the price,' said Martin.

'You seemed quite happy taking their coins,' said Shepherd.

'I don't think the Irish lot will leave me alone now. This is just a warning message,' said Martin.

'Well, it's your decision now then landlord, isn't it?' said Shepherd, harshly.

'Think my missus has made her mind up, she's packing already,' said Martin.

'In that case we'll bid you goodnight,' said Shepherd, walking off towards Abbey Street.

'That was a bit harsh,' said Perkins. 'He's got a wife and kids too, I suspect; yet the Micks have scared him off.'

'But Perkins, when you get close to rats, you catch their fleas. Sean Crowley said that he wanted to see the back of the rats and their fleas. This is just the start.'

'Is this a good thing or a bad thing?' said Perkins.

'It's never a good thing. Our Mr Crowley - if he's anything like his predecessor - Dubh O'Donnell, will have every business bowing down to him and paying into his empire, and very quickly. If they don't, they will get messages like Mr Martin has just had. The gang fights will stop, and the Irish will fall back to their old ways, and they fight themselves when there's nobody else to fight. You work it out.'

'And it stays the Rookeries and everything that it is feared for?' said Perkins.

'Absolutely' said Shepherd. 'We will still be hated, and distrusted, and we will be in the way of all the criminal activity, and so will be the subject of scare tactics. This isn't winning. It's not even drawing. This is a bit of a lull in proceedings.'

'You're starting to get like Sergeant Beddows,' said Perkins.

'I know now why he used to get so grumpy, coming down into this shithole,' said Shepherd.

'Cheer up, here's your mate Mr Crowley and his soldiers, come to gloat,' said Perkins, looking across towards Lower Green Street, where a crowd was assembled.

'Good evening, Constables Shepherd and...Perkins, I'm right, aren't I; Perkins, yes, I never forget a name. How are things with you gentlemen this evening?' said Crowley, smugly.

'Everyone seems pre-occupied, Mr Crowley. Have you heard that the incomers are on the move?' said Shepherd.

'So I've been told, Mr Shepherd. I hear some boys turned up in a Trojan horse and gave them a bit of a good hiding this morning?'

'What's this Trojan Horse everyone keeps going on about?' said Perkins.

'You should have got a better education, Mr Perkins. A wonderful tale, told to me many times by my Grandpa when I was a boy. It's about some brave Greek men, who hid away inside a wooden horse that was delivered to their enemies, the Trojans, as a free gift. The Trojans didn't suspect a thing, and the Greeks jumped out, sacked Troy and saw them all off. Very apt, don't you think?' said Crowley.

'I don't suppose you have heard who might have done it, Mr Crowley?' said Shepherd.

'I hear it was a butcher's wagon from Loughborough, and it was stolen. There's some bad boys over in Loughborough there are; railway workers and river and canal navies; big Irish blokes. I put money on the Londoners having crossed them at some time, and would be settling their score with them.'

'So none of your boys would be able to help us?' said Perkins.

'Cheeky young pup. My boys were keeping an eye out for me. I was outside the Gaol by eight o'clock, waiting to see my old folks. Looking quite well they are, for all Mr Shepherd's and Mr Beddows' best efforts last year,' said Crowley. 'You can check, honest'.

'I don't think we need to do that, Mr Crowley. It turns out that the men that were punished were all wanted for a number of serious crimes, including smashing up Cock Muck Hill,' said Shepherd.

'And murdering that old lady, do you mean?' said Crowley.

'Oh, she's not dead, but they didn't know that when they started grassing each other up,' said Shepherd. 'So they won't be in for quite as long as was thought, and when they get out, they'll be well pissed.'

'Well, I'll have to get some of my boys who are locked up to keep an eye out for them, and make sure they're looked after, inside,' said Crowley.

'I'm sure they'll like that. Your boys can perhaps help them get about, given they'll probably never walk again,' said Shepherd.

'God, that's terrible. That's the sort of thing that some of my republican friends get up to, allegedly, back in the Ole Country,' said Crowley.

'Is that so?' said Perkins. 'What a co-incidence.'

'A very effective way of putting terror in the hearts of men, so it is,' said Crowley.

'And how are your folk tonight, Mr Crowley?' said Shepherd.

'Very well Mr Shepherd. Some nice English gentlemen have just delivered a rather fine pig, to say 'thank-you' for something. They told us their folks were the ole ones in Cock Muck Hill. I think it was Mr Black himself who told me his Ma was still alive, before you just did. We are going to hang it up, and it will be perfect, roast on a spit, and our poor ones and children will have a feast.'

'That's very good of them. Our slaughter-men are good souls. I just hope they can afford to lose somebody's pig?' said Shepherd.

'They're very happy, and I've told them that we will keep an eye on their folk, being so close to our community,' said Crowley.

'So everyone seems happy with the outcome?' said Shepherd.

'Apart from the rats you mean, Constable Shepherd?' said Crowley, smiling.

'Yes, apart from the rats.'

'We're just going over to Cock Muck Hill ourselves,' said Shepherd. 'See how the old folks are.'

'Very nice too, Mr Shepherd. Have a nice cup of tea or two; enjoy the quiet while it lasts.'

'That sounds ominous, Mr Crowley?' said Shepherd.

'You know the Rookeries, Mr Shepherd. They'll soon be back to their good old ways. I'll be saying goodnight to you both, as I have a bottle of Ireland's finest waiting for me.'

'Goodnight, Mr Crowley,' said Shepherd, smiling.

*****

'So, all's well that ends well?' said Perkins.

'Just for the time being, Archie; make the most of it whilst it lasts.'

'So, do you think the Rookeries would be a good place for us to work, after all this?' said Shepherd.

'I love it, Shepherd. It's lively, it gets the blood pumping and it's interesting. I'd love to work down here all the time.'

'With your short fuse? The Irish will love you - given time,' said Shepherd.

'Do you think Mr Charters will leave us down here to get to grips with the area? It sounds like it's going to need it, if Mr Crowley and his boys are back in town?'

'We'll have to see what he says, when this finally settles down and the Rats have gone, once and for all. Now what about that cup of tea?'

'So long as it's drinkable, and not in glass jars,' said Perkins.

'Let's see who's about then,' said Shepherd, seeing that the yard appeared empty and the doors to the houses closed. The flicker of candles was evident in the small windows.

'What about old Mr Williams? Cheer him up and tell him he's going to get his medals back,' said Shepherd.

'Which one do I knock on?' said Perkins.

'That one straight in front of you. You'll have to knock hard as he's a bit deaf,' said Shepherd.

Perkins knocked hard on the new door; cheaply made, but sturdier than the last one the old man had to endure. There was no reply.

'Try again, one last time. He might have gone to bed,' said Shepherd.

Perkins banged hard again, as an even louder bang rang out, accompanied by a momentary bright flash.

Shepherd felt wet splashes over his face.

'What on earth was that, Archie?' said Shepherd.

Shepherd noticed that a large, round shaped hole had appeared in the door, directly in front of them, from which wisps of grey smoke now curled.

'Archie?'

Shepherd looked across at his colleague and saw that blood was spurting from a gaping wound in his throat and neck, just as Perkins fell to the floor.

'I'll finish you bastards off, try and rob an old soldier again!' came the cry as the door opened, and out protruded a smoking musket barrel, the gun held in the hands of poor old Mr Williams.

'Constable; I thought it were the robbers come back to finish me off,' said the ashen face old man, realising what he had just done.

Shepherd knelt down and placed his hand over Perkins' wound, but the pumping stopped, his eyes flickered, and Perkins drew his last breath.

*****

Glossary

There may be references or words used in this novella that require some level of clarification, so I have included a short glossary.

Abbey - A brothel or whore-house.
Almshouse - Provided as free accommodation for poorest of Parish.
Bruiser - A guard or protector for the members of 'The Fancy'.
Cab -Same meaning as an Abbey – a brothel or whore-house.
Ceili - Irish entertainment, normally comprising of singing & dancing. Also recorded as Ceilidh or Cailaigh in Victorian Leicester.
Chancer - Slang for an unscrupulous or dishonest opportunist who is prepared to try any dubious scheme for making money or furthering his own ends.
Chip-chopper - An odd job man.
Dudeen - Small, short clay pipe. Also recorded as Dudheen.
Fancy - The pugilists and followers of bare-knuckle fighting.
Greenceen - New Irish settlers looking for harvesting work.
Hawker - A person travelling door to door, town to town, selling small items such as matches, buttons, pins, etc.
Hunker – squat down, crouched.
Molly - A male homosexual.
Rookery - An area of high population and cramped accommodation. The Rookeries were the heart of Leicester's St Margaret's Parish.
Shillelagh - A bulbous ended Irish stick, cudgel or club.
Swag maker - Made the baskets for the Hawkers.

Other publications by Phil Simpkin

Jack Ketch's Puppets

http://www.amazon.co.uk/Jack-Ketchs-Puppets-
Introducing-
Borough/dp/1482712008/ref=sr_1_1?s=books&ie=UT
F8&qid=1364317134&sr=1-1

Leicestershire Myth & Legend – in verse

http://www.amazon.co.uk/Leicestershire-Myth-
Legend-Phil-
Simpkin/dp/1482566435/ref=sr_1_1?s=books&ie=UTF
8&qid=1364317251&sr=1-1

See Phil's website:

www.1455bookcompany.com

See 'The Borough Boys' Facebook Fan page:

https://www.facebook.com/pages/The-Borough-
Boys/368938166555376?ref=hl

Please note;-

**For those of you who are unfamiliar with the setting
in this series of novels and novellas, view my
'Borough Boys' page, where I describe them, at my
website-**

http://www.1455bookcompany.com/the-borough-
boys.html

Made in the USA
Charleston, SC
24 January 2014